IVY

A Journey Beyond the Imagination

SUSAN SHAKER

To my beloved angel brother, whose name was Saeed, who left this world when I was only seven and he was thirteen, and who continues to live in my heart every day.

Though he was just thirteen when he passed away, I learned more from him in those few years than words can ever express. Everyone loved him—so much so that when he died, neighbors from all around our home and my father's business came to his funeral. I still remember how he sat beside me at dinner, helping me eat like a playful child, and how he walked me to school each morning, always saying goodbye with, "See you after school."

He left us due to a doctor's mistreatment, and yet, for nearly thirty years, he returned to me in dreams—always in a white shirt and a beautiful smile, standing before a great gate framed by sky-tall green trees. I later learned that spirits are allowed to visit loved ones for thirty years before they cross over completely or are reborn. When the dreams stopped, I knew he had moved on.

During those years, many fortune tellers—though I never believed in them at first—told me I was being protected by a powerful presence. I began to believe it when I listened to stories of people who had a near-death experience (NDE). The other side is real. I know now that spirits walk among us, and when our time comes, we must account for our deeds before we return home, if we've lived well.

After he crossed, I faced hardship after hardship, and only then did I truly understand how deeply he had been protecting me. He was my only sibling. I miss him more than words can say, and I know with certainty that I'll see him again someday. Thanks for everything you did for me, my dear Saeed.

My dear brother Saeed,

I loved you then, my angel brother.
I love you now.
And I always will.

Acknowledgement

I would like to express my deepest gratitude to my beloved son, whose encouragement and unwavering belief in me have been my constant source of strength and light. To my friends and family, thank you for standing by me with patience, love, and support, even in the most challenging times. To my readers, your curiosity and openness give my stories life, and it is for you that I continue to write. Finally, I acknowledge the quiet moments of struggle and silence, for they became the soil from which these words were born.

Contents

CHAPTER ONE – Between Memory and Now

The cemetery was brimming with people—family, friends, faces both familiar and distant. The day was maddeningly beautiful, as if nature had chosen to mock her grief. The sun blazed in a clear blue sky, scattering diamonds across the lush, green grass. A gentle breeze whispered through the leaves, carrying scents of earth and blooms, coaxing the world toward celebration. But for Ivy, beauty had no place here. She was twenty-six, standing at the fragile edge of her own world.

At first glance, she could have been mistaken for any ordinary young woman—plain, unremarkable in the way strangers often are. But the moment she spoke, her voice had a way of owning the air, of drawing every gaze to her. Not today. Today, her voice was a low murmur buried in shadows.

She stood close to the grave's edge, her fingers locked around a folded note, the paper crumpled and soft from hours of restless clutching. The laughter of children drifted somewhere beyond the trees—light, pure, blissfully unaware. She didn't hear it. Her gaze never left the casket—wooden, polished, unbearably final—slowly vanishing beneath the weight of earth and a blanket of flowers.

Each bloom fell like a farewell, and each farewell landed on her chest. Beauty had turned against her, suffocating her. The petals whispered goodbye in silence so loud it stole her breath.

A breeze lifted her hair, gentle but deliberate, like the ghost of a hand she once knew. Her eyes fluttered shut. *His whisper.*

"You promised you'd always be here," she murmured, her voice cracking under the fragile weight of the words. The trees seemed to still, the air holding its breath to hear her.

People approached in murmuring waves, soft condolences spilling from their lips, hands brushing her shoulder with cautious kindness. She nodded, but her silence was heavy. Her words, once able to charm and move entire rooms, felt locked inside her ribs, too heavy to lift.

The world around her remained bright—birds sang, the grass glittered, but her heart was a house with every window boarded shut.

Her lips trembled as she whispered his name one last time.

When she finally looked around, she realized she was alone—everyone had gone except Liam.

"Let me take you home, Ivy," he said softly.

Her head snapped toward him, her eyes glassy, rimmed in red. Without a word, she swiped at her cheeks with a crumpled tissue, unaware that another presence had been at her side all along—her father, Cyrus—silent, steady, and watching.

Liam read her expression and stepped back, retreating into the periphery.

Ivy turned toward her car, each step an act of rebellion against the weight of her grief. She slid into the driver's seat, resting her head against the wheel. Her shoulders trembled.

Cyrus, a man in his late forties with thick, dark hair untouched by time, slid into the passenger seat. His hands rested quietly in his lap, his face calm but his eyes heavy with sadness.

"Sweetheart," he said gently, "take it easy. It breaks my heart to see you like this. Everything will be okay."

Her head snapped up, her voice flaring with raw anger. "He told me he'd always be with me! But he left me! He left me in this stupid world all alone!"

The words tore through the air like glass shattering.

She started the car. Cyrus placed a steady hand on her shoulder. "Honey… everything will be alright. I promise you that."

His voice was a salve, even as her pain kept bleeding.

The road blurred beneath her. Time felt suspended, as if she'd been driving for hours. She stopped only when the lake-shore appeared, its water a dark, restless mirror.

They walked side by side in silence until an old wooden bench came into view. Ivy paused, staring at it with eyes that seemed to be looking back in time.

"Do you remember, Dad?" she asked softly. "This was our spot. After biking, we'd sit here and watch the sunset."

Cyrus smiled faintly. "Of course, I remember. That was my favorite time in the world, being with you. You are my world, Ivy. And I promised your mother I'd always take good care of you."

Her chest rose with a shaky breath. "Dad! I'm going to miss this place. I'm going to miss you. I don't know how to live without you. I love you so much. And the crazy thing is—when I go home, I'll still expect you to be there."

She began to turn in place, taking in the lake, the trees, the fading light. "I don't know what to do. I always talked to you. Always. And now? You left me. You left me… left me… left me…"

The words dissolved into a whisper. She touched the bench as if it could anchor her and said, "Goodbye, Dad. I loved you… and I will love you until the day I see you again."

She walked away, each step another piece of her breaking.

Cyrus remained seated, watching her go. "I love you too, my sweetheart. You rocked my world… but I didn't leave you."

He turned away, and as he stepped into the breeze, his form began to shimmer, soft light replacing flesh, until he dissolved completely, leaving only a faint rainbow shimmer drifting in the air.

Ivy turned back, her eyes catching the glint. "It's just my imagination," she whispered. And then she left.

The next morning, Ivy woke into a silence so heavy it felt alive. The house was wrapped in stillness, as if even the walls were mourning.

Mornings used to greet her with the earthy scent of fresh coffee and the quiet scrape of her father's chair against the floor as he waited for her at the kitchen table, smiling that calm, steady smile. Now, there was only the dull hum of the refrigerator and the hollow ache of absence.

She lay in bed far too long, the weight of the blankets pressing her down like a second grief. When she finally rose, she moved through her morning like a shadow, shower, clothes, keys, carefully avoiding her gaze in the mirror, avoiding the kitchen entirely, as though stepping into that space without him would be betrayal.

Work offered no real refuge. Her office felt airless. She sat behind her desk, her gaze fixed through the glass wall at the endless blur of colleagues moving in the hallway, faces without names, colors without meaning.

The door creaked open. Emma stepped inside, her smile as warm as a patch of sunlight in winter. She was shorter than Ivy, her hair catching the light like spun gold, her presence carrying a quiet goodness that Ivy had always trusted.

"Ivy!" Emma's voice was gentle but bright. "We're heading to yoga. Come with us. You need peace more than anyone right now."

Ivy barely turned her head, her eyes glassy and distant. Emma's lips moved, but her words were muffled, as though they came through water.

"What?" Ivy asked softly, her voice stripped of energy.

Emma moved closer, took her hand. "Exactly my point. Come on. Let me help you breathe again."

The words hit wrong. Ivy's chest tightened. "How can you possibly know what I'm going through?" Her voice rose, trembling with pain. "Your mother's still alive. You have brothers who care for you. My mother's been gone for years. My brother died because of hospital negligence. And now my father, the only one I had left, is gone. Don't tell me you understand. Don't compare your life to mine."

Emma flinched, but not from offense, from love. She didn't speak.

The weight of her own cruelty struck Ivy instantly. Guilt swept through her like nausea. Without a word, she pushed past Emma and hurried to the restroom, the cold tiles greeting her with their indifferent chill. Her forehead pressed against the wall, her voice breaking. "I miss you, Dad… I miss you. But I can't hurt my friends."

The door opened softly. Emma crossed the space without hesitation and wrapped Ivy in her arms.

"I don't feel what you feel, Ivy," she whispered. "I know your pain is sky high. But I understand in my own way. You're like the sister I never had. Let me help you."

Her voice wrapped around Ivy like a blanket.

"How about this?" Emma continued. "Come to yoga. You don't have to move a muscle. Just sit, breathe. And after, come to my mom's. Everyone will be there—it's Friday. My mom insists. She says the table feels empty without you."

For the first time in days, Ivy let out a trembling laugh. "Okay," she whispered.

The yoga center was bathed in soft light and the perfume of calming oils. Ivy took a spot against the wall, knees drawn up, her gaze drifting over the slow, graceful movements of the others. The music was a low hum, the instructor's voice an even softer tide.

Her thoughts slipped away from the present, sliding toward the memory of her father, his voice in the kitchen, warm hands around a coffee cup. It felt so real, she almost smiled.

Then, "I… v… y…"

Her name floated through the air, breaking the illusion. She blinked, returning to the room. Every pair of eyes was on her. Anger flared briefly—she had been *there* with him. Now, she was here again.

The instructor's eyes stayed on her as she turned to Emma. "Who was she? She must be an expert in yoga."

Emma shook her head, still caught off guard. "No, that was her first time."

The studio air seemed to vibrate with unasked questions. The instructor's gaze lingered on Ivy, curious, a little in awe. Emma stood caught between pride and protectiveness, and Ivy, suddenly visible to everyone, felt the afterglow of that other world fade from her skin. She offered a thin, apologetic smile, gathered herself with quiet dignity, and slipped out.

She moved through the evening like a ghost. Streets unspooled beneath her shoes; the city breathed around her without touching her. By the time she reached home, the walls had settled into their new, unbearable shape. She didn't turn on the lights. Shadow suited the room, and the room suited her.

She drifted to the kitchen and stopped at the invisible boundary where memory began: his chair, the light that used to slant across the table, the way a coffee cup had sounded when he set it down, soft and sure. Her hands hovered over drawers and cabinets as if touching wood might conjure him. Nothing answered. Quiet folded over quiet until it felt like drowning.

It broke out of her like a storm. "Come on, Dad! I saw you. Come on!" Her voice cracked the way glass seams crack, hairline first, then all at once. She slid down the cupboard and let grief take her, shaking her to the floor. "Please… please, Dad…"

A knock struck the door, one clean sound, too real to be memory. Hope flared so violently it hurt. She ran, breath hitching, heart stuttering. She wrenched the door open and froze.

Liam filled the frame, tall, certain, the neat line of his uniform catching the hall light. His hazel eyes, flecked like warm honey, softened when they met her ruined face. "Hey, you," he murmured, the low warmth of his voice a familiar hand reaching across a gulf. "I couldn't wait any longer."

She searched behind him anyway. Empty hallway. Empty air. The hope fell without a sound.

"What is it? Why are you here?" The flatness of her tone surprised even her.

Concern pulled tight across his features. He stepped inside, closed the door with a certainty that made the room feel smaller and safer. "Ivy, what's going on? You haven't answered. I haven't seen you since the funeral."

"My phone is off." She folded her arms as if to hold herself in. "I've been working. What do you want?"

He took her by the forearms gently, not to restrain but to steady. "I'm worried about you." His voice sank low, controlled. "You can't shut everyone out. We all, sooner or later, we all have to say goodbye."

She held his gaze until the words landed, until the last of them stopped vibrating in the air. When she spoke, it was almost a passing of sentence. "Good," she murmured. "Good if I go, too." The cold honesty of it frightened them both. "I never asked to be here. I never wanted any of this. If God took everyone I love, why should I care what He wants?" Her eyes brightened with a grief that had teeth. "He can have it back. This precious life. He can take it now."

The silence that followed was the deep kind—the kind that measures distances between people and dares them to cross. Liam crossed. He wrapped her carefully, as though she might splinter if he pressed too hard, and he anchored her to the earth with the simple fact of his breath.

"I don't know the right words," he said into her hair. "I don't. I'm confused, too. But I know this: do not hand your faith to pain. Don't let it eat the part of you that still remembers morning. Time won't fix everything. It never does. But it dulls the blade. It lets you carry what you couldn't lift. Hold on. Just hold on."

She broke then, not quietly. The sound was raw and human and sacred, and he stood for it, rocked her through it with the patience of someone willing to be a shelter even in the storm he can't stop. Outside, dusk deepened until the windows became mirrors. Inside, the kitchen absorbed everything and offered nothing back but space.

Morning offered a trick. The fragrance of coffee ran ahead of her into the hall. Hope, reckless and bright, sprinted after it. She burst into the kitchen with a child's certainty. "I knew it—" The word died when she saw Liam by the counter, smiling that soft, tired smile of a man who'd studied all night for a test he hadn't known he'd take.

"I made breakfast," he said, and the gentleness in it wasn't pity. "Stay. Eat with me."

The disappointment buckled her knees for a heartbeat, but she leaned into him instead. "Okay," she breathed, surrendering to the ordinary—the plate, the steam, the quiet clink of fork against ceramic. They ate like people building a bridge with tiny motions: bite by bite, breath by breath. When she finally looked up and let a small, real smile be seen, Liam held it in his chest as if it were proof of something worth fighting for.

"Thank you," she said.

"For what?"

"For not leaving."

The day moved under her with less resistance. Grief stayed, it always would, but it stopped dragging at her ankles. At work, Emma appeared in the doorway like a steady lighthouse, checking in with a glance, a joke, a careful ease that asked nothing and offered much.

"Lunch?" Emma leaned on the frame, grin crooked. "The café with the good coffee."

"Why not," Ivy said, and meant it.

They sat in the corner booth where sunlight pooled across the table and turned the steam from their cups into small ghosts. Emma watched her with obvious relief. "Would you come to yoga again? I... just because I like you there."

Ivy's fork paused midair. The twitch across her features was small but real. "It's not for me," she said, soft but settled. "I'm sorry."

Emma squeezed her hand without letting disappointment touch her voice. "No worries. I get it."

They let silence be kind to them, then collected small stories and old laughter like coins from a jar. When Ivy laughed for real, quick and bright, Emma blinked hard and looked away, pretending not to wipe her eye.

"Same time next week?" Emma asked as they stood.

"Yeah," Ivy said. "I'd like that."

Days learned to walk again. Ivy let them. Routine laid down rails, and the train of her life, damaged as it was, began to move. Emma remained in a warm orbit. Liam threaded quiet into her hours—a note on her desk, a favorite tea placed within reach, the discipline to say nothing when silence did the work.

And yet. Some nights, the air changed. She would be walking home beneath an obedient row of streetlights when the world would tilt, almost imperceptibly, toward watchfulness. Her skin would know it first, the prickle along the forearms, the instinct that makes prey pause.

The message arrived on such a night.

Ivy.

Just her name. No number she recognized. No punctuation. A single syllable hung in the glow of her screen like a bead of mercury.

Her breath shortened. She spun slowly under the streetlamp, searching doorways, alleys, the dark glass of a parked car. No one. Nothing. Only the skitter of leaves along concrete, the hiss of far-off tires. She could have blocked the number. Every nerve screamed for it. But reason, cold, careful, laid a hand on her wrist. If it happens again, you'll want proof.

She saved the contact as Unknown and walked home faster, keys between her fingers, gaze slicing the dark into pieces she could survive. Inside, locks slid, bolts seated. The message remained, a wolf track in new snow: small, perfect, undeniable.

The next afternoon, she told Liam in a park where the paths were strewn with leaves like spent gold. His face changed shape as she spoke; concern pulled the lines taut, and something older, protectiveness, settled in behind his eyes.

"Stay at my place," he said simply. "For a bit. Till I sort this, let me see the number."

She opened her phone with hands that didn't feel like hands, scrolled to Unknown, and tapped. The screen offered her emptiness. No record. No number. No message.

"It was there," she whispered, the humiliation of doubt mixing with fear. "I saved it."

"Are you sure?" He caught himself, softened it. "Phones glitch. Burners evaporate. Next time, screenshot it. Please."

"I will." The promise steadied her breath.

He brushed an errant thread of hair from her cheek with the back of his fingers. "Be careful," he said, and the brief touch said the rest.

But the unease didn't leave. It learned her shadows, waited in her mirrors. It followed her to the threshold of sleep and perched there, patient as an owl.

It followed her, too, back to the studio when she surprised Emma at her office door and said, "I want to come again. Just to watch." Relief broke across Emma's face like the sun, pure and uncomplicated.

The studio welcomed them with candle-warmth and that familiar, impossible peace. Ivy stood by the wall, arms loosely crossed, heartbeat skittish. The room settled, bodies arranged themselves into calm geometry, breath lifted and lowered like a tide. The instructor's voice laid a path through stillness.

Ivy scanned the soft-dark, certain of nothing except the ache in her chest. Then she saw him. Not a face, not details, only the fact of him: a tall presence where no one had been a moment before, occupying the far corner as if corners had been invented to hold him.

She blinked. Emptiness blinked back.

A thread of cold slipped down her spine. She moved without sound between mats, toward the corner where the air felt denser, haunted. The empty mat was indented, the way a pillow remembers a head. She touched it. Warm.

"Ivy?" Emma's whisper tugged her to the surface. She stood too quickly. "I thought I saw someone." Her voice made it true and not true at once.

"Maybe the calm is playing tricks," Emma said, but the worry in her eyes said she believed Ivy more than she believed calm.

Ivy sat beside her, but the room had changed. The edges of everything had sharpened. The mirrors held too many versions of her. The minutes stretched wax-thin, quiet and flammable.

At the closing chime, before gratitude could ripple through the room, Ivy was already up. "Something came up," she told Emma, brittle and apologetic. "I'll call you tomorrow." She fled into the night like a deer startled by a snap of twigs.

Cold met her at the door; she welcomed it. She drove without a destination, as if movement itself were protection, as if speed could outrun the question beating under her ribs, *Was it him? Was it grief? Was it something else?*

The city smeared into streamers of gold and red. She turned down a quieter road, a reflex born of the need to breathe. The asphalt narrowed, hedged in by sleeping houses. A bend. A dark. And then, a shape that did not belong there.

A pickup truck loomed broadside across the road, dead-eyed, a black animal sprawled in the lane. She hit the brake. The scream of tires tore through the night. Time thin-stretched. Sound rearranged itself into single notes: a gasp, a prayer, the metallic crescendo of impact. Glass burst, a thousand bright stars. The seat-belt caught, bruising; the world inverted and went away.

The first man on scene was the truck's owner, called from near-sleep by the unholy sound of fate choosing a spot on his street. He ran barefoot, phone in hand, and stopped at the edge of wreckage because there are distances even urgency respects.

"What the hell?" He didn't finish. The word collapsed under the sight.

"911," he told his phone, and then he told the night, and then he told the operator, voice shaking but holding. "There's been a bad crash. Send everyone. Fire, ambulance, she's pinned."

Sirens learned the route to his house in minutes. Red-blue washed the quiet facades of homes, turned windows into emergency paintings. Firefighters flowed out with that terrifying grace of people who do very hard things on purpose. Police set lines, kept neighbors on porches. Paramedics knelt in the glass and called the driver "ma'am" because dignity is medicine.

An officer drew the truck owner aside, clipboard angled, pen ready. "Where were you when it happened?"

"Home. Getting ready for bed." The man stared at the ruin, as if naming his location might make a more sensible story out of what had just occurred.

"Truck was parked?"

"Right there." He pointed, helpless. "She just came out of nowhere. This is a dead end. How—"

The officer wrote what could be written and let the rest sit unanswerable in the air. "Do you know the driver?"

The man's laugh was brittle with disbelief. "No. I don't know her."

Behind them, the hydraulics hissed and growled. Steel surrendered. Hands in heavy gloves did delicate work. A medic leaned in close to the slack face, eyes narrowing, voice low and practiced. "Ma'am? Can you hear me? Sternal rub." No response. They traded looks that people learn to read only by surviving the reading.

A white sheet came out, but it hovered, uncertain, like a cloud that refused to settle. A finger moved. Small as a sparrow's heartbeat, but real.

"Hold up." Everything reversed in a breath. Oxygen. Lines. Numbers. Commands that were prayers and vice versa. They opened a path where no path had been. They argued with the darkness on her behalf and, inch by inch, they won enough ground to keep arguing.

Thirty minutes later, the wreckage released her. She left it strapped and braced, a fragile traveler returned from too far away. "We've got a pulse," someone said, and the words went down the line like light.

"Name?" an officer asked another, already riffling gently through a small purse, a jacket's inner pocket. The question felt embarrassingly intimate under the floodlights.

They found her phone. Locked. A case with a hairline crack. A few IDs: the kind we offer the world to prove we exist. A driver's license. A photo of a girl who looked like Ivy on a day she'd slept well. The officer said her name aloud, once, to test the shape of it.

"Ivy," he read, and glanced up at the paramedic, who nodded as if names were anchors that keep souls from drifting too far.

They slid her into the ambulance. Doors closed with a hollow, decisive sound. The siren rose, a long, keening thread, and the vehicle shot forward, pulling the night open ahead of it.

Later, much later, a hospital would label it: they brought her back; she slipped away again into a different kind of distance. Not gone. Not here. Coma is a country that does not grant visas easily.

In the blank hours after, officers stood in the coiled quiet of the ER corridor and finished the work of the living: forms, calls, the ritual of contact. One of them opened her phone again out of habit, thumb moving where muscle memory says it should. The lock screen lit: a wallpaper of a shoreline at dusk. No message notifications. No missed calls. Nothing but her name, the time, and the quiet insistence of the battery icon.

If a message had been there, it was not there now.

Back on the street, the truck owner stood in his robe and watched a tow pull warped metal away from the spot where ordinary life had split. He wrapped his arms around himself and tried, and failed, to recall what the night had felt like before the sound. Somewhere, a light in a bedroom went out. Somewhere else, one flicked on.

And in a room that hummed the steady music of machines, Ivy lay very still. If you watched long enough, you could see the chest rise. If you were very quiet, you could hear that life still insisted on being counted. On a small table, someone had placed the folded note found in her coat pocket. The creases were soft with handling. The edges wore the history of hours. The first line, visible where the fold didn't quite meet, read like a promise that had become a prayer:

I'll meet you where the light begins.

CHAPTER TWO – Into the Unseen

Ivy stood frozen, the night around her thinned and sharpened, as if the world had been cut from glass. Her car lay twisted just yards away, metal buckled like folded paper, windshield star-burst into a thousand glittering wounds. Steam hissed from the ruptured hood; the air stank of coolant, hot rubber, and something scorched. A man, barefoot, frantic, was sprinting toward the wreck, panic etched deep into every line of his face.

"Sir, I'm okay!" Ivy called, her voice steady, her confusion louder. He didn't even glance at her.

"I said I'm fine! Could you at least call me a cab?" She stepped directly into his path, palms up, an immovable fact.

He ran through her.

Cold sprinted up her spine, an arctic rush, weightless and bottomless, leaving her breathless without needing breath. She staggered back, staring at her hands as they trembled in a way that was more light than flesh.

"I am hallucinating again," she whispered. But the words had no anchor. Somewhere deeper than fear, the truth had already found her.

Drawn by a certainty she couldn't name, Ivy moved to the wreck and leaned over the torn frame. Her gaze fell into the driver's seat.

Her own body slumped there, blood darkening her hairline, skin too pale beneath the smear of glass dust, lashes still as ash. The seatbelt cut across her chest like a rude, saving hand. Her mouth parted soundlessly. The world tilted; a cold wave of terror broke over her and kept breaking.

"No… no, this isn't happening." She stepped back, the night widening around her, her heart hammering even though, somewhere, another heart had stopped.

She spun and froze.

Through a thinning mist stood a tall figure bathed in soft light, as if dawn had chosen only him. The glow did not glare; it welcomed. Familiarity moved toward her before his face did an old safety, a homecoming carried in the set of his shoulders. Then the features came clear: the gentle strength of his jaw, the eyes she had ached for across so many mornings.

Her knees nearly gave. *It can't be…*

He smiled, and the years between them dissolved. He opened his arms as naturally as breathing.

"My sweetheart Ivy," Cyrus whispered, the love in his voice warm enough to thaw any winter.

She couldn't move. Shock, fear, hope, disbelief—each surged forward, collided, and stalled inside her chest. Her lips parted, but sound refused the edge of the world.

Cyrus did not rush. He only stood, arms open, the same patient father he had always been, his smile steady and sure—as though he had been waiting in that light since the first moment she learned to say his name.

Ivy's eyes filled, bright as glass about to spill. "Dad...?" she breathed, hardly trusting the sound.

Still unsure whether this was mercy or a cruel mirage, she took one careful step, then another. With each pace, warmth gathered around her like sunlight after a storm, familiar, protective, impossibly gentle. The moment the distance vanished, she broke with a choked sob and fell into his arms. They closed around her solid anchoring, real as gravity and banishing doubt like mist at noon.

"My brave, beautiful Ivy," Cyrus murmured, his voice steady and overflowing with love.

"Dad?" Her voice cracked; the dam gave way. "I thought you left me. I didn't know how to breathe without you. I missed you so much."

Tears streamed as she held him as if the world might steal him again. Cyrus stroked her hair with that old, quiet rhythm that had once calmed nightmares.

"I know, my sweet Ivy. I missed you, too." His tone softened with ache. "But you thought I left you? I never did. I walked beside you every step. I tried to reach you, to ease what I could... but from here, not every bridge holds."

She pulled back, searching his face as her gaze swept the silvered air around them. "Is this... after death?" she whispered. "Am I dead?"

"Yes… and no," he said, grave and tender. "You are standing at the first threshold—the space between. We haven't crossed fully. You are not dead, Ivy. You must go back."

Her heart sank like a stone. "No," she pleaded, shaking her head, clutching his wrists. "I won't. I want to stay with you."

Sorrow welled in his eyes as he cradled her face. "My darling girl… it isn't your time. Your road is unfinished. I know the walking hurts, but you are bound by purpose. There is more in you that the world still needs."

Her gaze drifted into the pale horizon, then returned, fragile with longing. "Dad… can I see Mom? And Finn?"

Cyrus's expression softened into a bittersweet smile. He brushed away a tear with his thumb. "My sweetheart, they've gone farther on, beyond where I am. I haven't seen them yet. When I cross fully, I will." His eyes flickered with hope and sadness together. "But you… you are not meant to follow us. Not yet."

A voice uncoiled softly through the mist, "You can stay for a while."

Ivy glanced around, startled. "Really?" she whispered, hope flaring like a struck match.

Cyrus's expression hardened; his voice cut cleanly through the silvered air. "Not now, Ethan. Stop. Go away."

Ivy's brows knit. Only then did she notice the figure at his side, a man shorter than Cyrus, slender, almost delicate, his presence quiet but strangely concentrated, like a drawn bow. He stood a pace back, saying nothing, watching everything.

"Dad… who is he?" Ivy asked, voice low.

"He's nobody," Cyrus answered too quickly.

The man, Ethan, shook his head once, slowly. The look he leveled at Cyrus carried disappointment, warning, and something like a plea.

Before Cyrus could speak again, the stranger stepped forward. His eyes, luminous with an intensity that felt out of place in such soft light, fixed on Ivy. "When did you die?" he asked, blunt as a bell.

Cyrus didn't turn to him. "She's not dead," he said, calm and unyielding. "She's in a coma… and she has to go back."

Pain shadowed Ivy's face. "Dad, I'm not going back." Her voice trembled, the words pulled straight from the ache. "There's nothing for me to return to."

Cyrus closed the distance and gathered her in, his embrace a quiet command. "You have to," he whispered, insistence wrapped in love.

Ethan pivoted away and strode toward the scene where paramedics worked the wreck, where gloved hands labored over the body that wore Ivy's face. He folded his arms, mouth tilting into a sneer that didn't quite reach his eyes. "See?" he said to no one and everyone. "She's dead. No heartbeat, no breathing, nothing."

The monitor erupted into sharp, insistent beeping.

Ethan exhaled, long-suffering. "Ah… never mind," he said, flat as paper, and drifted back through the thinning veil until he stood before Ivy once more. "What is your name?" he asked, gaze now gentler, measuring.

"Ivy," she said softly. She studied him, his slight frame, the unnerving steadiness in his eyes and frowned. "When did you die?"

A small, wry smile touched his mouth. "I'm not dead," he replied. "I'm alive and healthy."

Ivy narrowed her eyes, confusion tightening in her chest. "Then how come you're not dead… but you're here?"

The light around him seemed to tilt, as if deciding what it would show and what it would keep.

Ethan's mouth tilted, the chuckle low and wrong in so quiet a place. "Good question, sweetheart. I've trained myself to separate my soul from my body. While my body rests, my soul wanders."

Bewildered, Ivy turned toward her father. "Is he real?" The moment the words left her, her voice rippled and thinned, an echo thrown into a hollow sky.

Everything lurched.

Weight, heat, the harsh bite of air in lungs—reality slammed back into her like a door on a storm. Her eyes flew open. A raw, animal sound tore from her. "Noooo… please send me back, let me go!" She thrashed, limbs fighting the belts and hands that held her. "Please!"

"Easy, don't fight, you'll hurt yourself," a paramedic said, urgent and kind. Another voice counted, "Breath sounds present, hold her there, watch the line." But nothing on Earth could comfort what she had just lost.

The room fractured. The stretcher below her blurred into glass and light. And then she rose again, weightless, breathless, hovering over the pale, frantic body that wore her face. The sight jolted her, electric and impossible.

She lifted her gaze.

Cyrus stood before her, warmth steadying the cold churn of the scene below. Ethan was gone, as if dawn had erased him.

"Dad," she gasped, hands reaching, soul aching open. "Do you know how he could do that?"

Cyrus's eyes darkened with worry. "Ivy! Why would you even want to know that?"

Her longing cracked her clean through. Tears streamed over a face that was almost not a face at all. She reached for him, fingers trembling in the space that refused to hold them. "Dad! I want to see you every day or at least every night when my body rests. I can't live like this. I'm going mad. I'll hurt myself just to find my way back. I need you… I can't lose you again!"

His lips parted, then the ether shivered, as if a veil were stirred by an unseen hand.

Ethan stood there again, silent, ghost-like, hands tucked in his pockets as though this in-between were a park he knew well. Ivy whirled toward him, urgency taut as wire. "Ethan… tell me. Explain how you're able to do this."

He smiled, slow and knowing. "Now you're serious," he teased, velvet-smooth. "I like it."

She drifted closer despite the tug of her body below, her outline flickering with the strain. "Please… tell me how. I want to see my father again. On Earth, it's impossible. But here, here I can. Please."

Ethan glanced down at the stretcher, at the pale face, the trembling lashes, the frantic ballet of hands and instruments and numbers. His expression sobered. "You're about to snap back any second," he said gently. "The thread is tightening."

"Please," Ivy begged, fists clasped at her chest, the last word ripping out of her like a cry from a breaking soul. "Tell me before it happens. Please!"

Cyrus stepped in, voice low and fierce. "Enough. She is not crossing any farther. Not like this."

Ethan's eyes met Cyrus's, warning, sorrow, something like respect passing between them. Then he looked back at Ivy and softened.

"What I do," he said, "is not a trick. It is a vow. Doors like this take something, and not all of it returns the same. If you force them, they take more." He lifted a hand, hesitant, and hovered his fingertips a breath from her brow. "But if you must have a compass, take only this: when the world goes thin and sleep lifts like a tide, listen for the hush between your breaths. That quiet seam? That is the hinge. Stand there. Be still. Do not push. If the way opens, it opens to you, never the other way around."

"Ivy, no," Cyrus warned. "There is a cost."

Ethan's hand never quite touched her, yet warmth pooled across her forehead as if light itself had traced a sign there. "If you ever hear three soft knocks from nowhere," he murmured, "do not answer the first. Wait for the second to pass. Meet the third with courage, or not at all."

The stretcher below jerked; the monitor stuttered, then climbed. "She's back, hold her, prep two milligrams," a voice called.

The pull became a riptide.

Cyrus cupped her face, and for one impossible instant, his hands were as real as the word *home*. "My darling girl," he whispered, the love in it vast enough to span whatever this place was. "Not yet. Finish your road. I'll be where the light begins."

"Dad..." she breathed.

The world seized her and did not ask permission. Sound swelled; pain arrived with edges; gravity laid its claim. She slammed back into herself. Hands held her; a mask descended; a cool wave slid up her arm.

"Easy. You're okay. Stay with us."

Her lashes fluttered. Shapes trembled, then smeared. Somewhere, someone said her name like a promise: "Ivy."

Darkness gathered, not the cruel kind, but the deep, muffled quiet of a room behind a door that would open again. Machines took up their patient hymn.

On the other side of the hush, in the space between memory and now, a faint pattern of warmth lingered on her brow, like the echo of three distant knocks waiting in a future night.

Ethan's smile deepened, the edges of him shimmering like mist caught in moonlight. He leaned in, eyes sharp and kind at once, fixing on Ivy's flickering presence. "Do you know anything about yoga?" he asked, as if offering a riddle a child could answer.

Ivy blinked, thrown by the question. Impatience thinned her voice. "My friend… she goes to classes. But what does that have to do with separating the spirit from the body?"

Cyrus stood at her side, brow furrowed, worry and curiosity braided tight. Ethan's grin widened. The air thickened, the space between worlds seemed to pulse, as if knowledge were dancing just beyond reach.

He chuckled softly, a low, musical ripple through the void. "Ah, Ivy… yoga isn't stretching and sunshine," he said, voice lowering to a reverent hush. "The ancient practice was built to loosen the boundary between body and spirit. The masters learned to slip the tether, ride the astral currents, and return."

Ivy stared, wide-eyed, her outline guttering as the pull of her body gathered strength. "You mean… you use yoga to leave your body?"

Ethan nodded slowly. "A disciplined form. Years. Breath, stillness, attention. Learning to quiet the prison of flesh until it becomes a dock and you, the sea. Then you go, and you come back." His gaze softened as he took in her trembling light. "You're close, but untrained. That's why you're being dragged back. Your time here is almost gone."

Ivy shook her head violently, tears of luminous silver streaking down her translucent cheeks. "No… no, please, teach me! Even if I can only see him once in a while… I'll do anything." The space around them pulsed, a heartbeat made of light. Her outline thinned, flickering, while faint through the veil came the frantic calls of paramedics repeating her name as if it were a rope they could throw across worlds.

Ethan's expression sobered, understanding how near the thread was to snapping. He stepped closer; his glow brightened even as his form slipped like smoke through her desperate reach. His voice, once crisp, now wavered, warped and distant, as though rising from the floor of an endless sea. "For the last time, Ivy…" the words stretched thin, "Come and… find me… I'll teach you…"

"I can't hear you, Ethan!" Panic blazed in her eyes. Sound twisted, muffled; she was sinking, sinking, the pull of flesh dragging her down. "Ethan… Ethan!" she cried, but her voice broke into nothing, scattered and swallowed by the returning dark. She reached out; her hands passed straight through his dissolving light.

The last thing she saw was Ethan's silhouette unraveling into the mist, one arm still outstretched, the shape of a promise suspended between worlds. Then the connection tore.

A violent jolt. The ether vanished. White light exploded over her, harsh, clinical, while metal clanged and wheels squealed and human voices snapped into command.

Ivy gasped; fire filled her lungs. She was back.

A warm, solid hand gripped hers hard, anchoring her to the noise and weight of the room. Not Ethan. A paramedic, brow furrowed, jaw set, held her steady. "Hold her!" he barked. "Keep her still, don't let the IV pull out!"

The needle's sting carved through the fading warmth like a shard of winter. Her body felt strange and heavy, a suit she didn't remember putting on. Blood crept back through the line, slow, reluctant, proof of the world reclaiming her, inch by inch, from the edge where her father waited and Ethan had stood.

Her lips parted, trembling, a breath more prayer than sound. "Ethan…" she whispered into the sterile air.

Only the machines answered, steady, indifferent, alive.

The sterile chill pressed against her skin like invisible weights. Ivy lay motionless beneath the blaze of white light, the heaviness of flesh unbearable after the weightless hush of the other side. The monitor kept its indifferent rhythm, beep, pause, beep, time measured in cold increments that did not care whether she stayed or slipped away.

She turned her head a fraction. Uniforms, wires, chrome, blur into blur. Her throat worked around a whisper that hardly became sound. "Ethan…" Nothing answered. No thrum of warmth. Only the dull ache of existence and the hard, foreign bite of the IV.

Panic rose clean and merciless, a tide that didn't ask permission. *Was it real? Was he real?* The last image, the outstretched hand in the light, burned at the edges of her vision, already fraying like a dream that refuses to be held. *Find me… I'll teach you…* The words slid across her mind, slick and beautiful and slipping away.

I have to find him. The thought struck like a nail. Her fingers curled weakly in the sheets, a tiny rebellion against gravity. *I will find him. I have to go back. There has to be a way.*

She shut her eyes and hunted the seam Ethan had named—the hush between breaths, the thin hinge where the world goes quiet. Inhale. The world arrived, heavy. Exhale. A hairline crack opened, fragile, almost nothing. She waited there, trembling, refusing to push, as if brute wanting might scare it closed.

A shadow leaned into the light. "Ivy?" A nurse, gentle and brisk at once. "You're safe. Try not to move." Fingers checked the line, smoothed tape against her arm. Someone else adjusted a monitor; paper rustled; shoes whispered over tile. The human choreography of keeping a body.

Again. Inhale. Weight returned. Exhale. There, the thinness, the soft door, just beginning to consider her. She hovered at its threshold, desperate and still. Her pulse, traitor and savior, beat against the quiet like a fist on glass.

Footsteps hurried near the curtain. A low voice, authority softened by concern. "How's she doing?" A reply in numbers and acronyms. Names moved around her like buoys: O_2, IV, CT. She clung to the small, private silence between the syllables, memorizing the shape of it.

Her lips barely moved. "Dad…" The word broke on her tongue, raw as a first step after a fall. The room did not change, but something in her steadied. The vow sharpened until it felt like steel under her skin: she would learn. Breath by breath, she would make her body a dock and her soul the sea. She would find the hinge in the dark and wait for the third soft knock.

A new warmth touched her hand, bigger, rougher, familiar. "Ivy." The voice came from the doorway, frayed with fear and relief at once. Liam. The name rose inside her like heat. She turned her head a fraction more; his outline filled the blur, broad shoulders, those hazel eyes rimmed in sleepless worry.

"I'm here," he said, the words a quiet anchor. His thumb brushed the back of her hand as if reminding the blood which direction to flow. "You're okay. Stay with me."

She wanted to say *I have to go back* and *I won't leave you* in the same breath. Instead, her gaze held his, and she let the meaning live there: *I'm here for now.*

The beeping held its stubborn rhythm. Machines breathed their patient hymn. Somewhere beyond the fluorescent ceiling and the clean sting of antiseptic, a lighter place waited at the edge of sleep. Ivy closed her eyes and folded the memory of Ethan's outstretched arm into the safest corner of herself.

I will find you, she promised the dim, secret place between one breath and the next. *And when the door opens, I'll know.*

A hot tear slid down her cheek as she stared at the blank ceiling, heart cleaved between two worlds, knowing she had only just begun to grasp the impossible road ahead.

The soft creak of the door cut through the sterile hum. She barely managed to turn her head, but the presence that entered brought a gentle warmth to the room had not known. Quiet, purposeful footfalls; the hush of fabric; the faint scent of cold air and aftershave. A uniformed officer knelt beside her bed, his strong hand, trembling, finding hers. For a heartbeat, she flinched, a wild hope sparking that it might be Ethan; then reality settled like a cool cloth.

His expression was raw, relief, tenderness, sleepless fear laid bare. With unexpected gentleness, he brushed the tear from her cheek. "Ivy…" he whispered, voice thick with emotion. "I'm here. I'm so happy you survived. Please, get well soon." It was Liam.

He leaned in and pressed a soft, lingering kiss to her damp forehead, his breath a fragile warmth against the chill of the room. One hand threaded tenderly through her tangled hair, smoothing it back as if to shield her from the harshness of what waited beyond these walls. The monitors kept their patient hymn; the IV line pulsed cool against her skin.

Ivy closed her eyes beneath his touch. For one borrowed breath, the wreckage inside her eased, the fractured edges aligning. But under that brief calm, the ache for her father and for the echo of Ethan's outstretched hand burned on, bright and undiminished, like a star she could feel even through the glare of hospital lights.

Days bled into nights, nights unspooled into weeks, and Ivy drifted through them, half tide, half ember, held together by pain and a thin, stubborn thread of will. Healing did not so much arrive as grind forward: millimeters, then inches. The fog of weakness lifted by fractions until, one morning, the simple act of sitting upright felt like a small rebellion against gravity. She shook with the effort, fragile but defiant, her breath a measured count against the ache.

The room became a slow carousel of faces and flowers. Friends, coworkers, even the almost-familiar from the edges of her life filed past bearing cards, daisies, chocolates wrapped in nervous crinkles. Their smiles tried to float; their eyes could not hide the shock of how pale she'd become, how hollow the bones made her look. They spoke gently, too gently, as if the air around her might shatter. They came and went like shadows at sundown, kind, sincere, and gone.

One presence did not blur. Liam. Night after night, without fail, his boots found the same path to her door. He took the chair beside her bed as if it had been made for him, set his cap on his knee, and wove quiet into the sterile hum. When sleep refused her, he read in a low voice, pages turning like soft wings. When her arms trembled at the simple lift of a brush, he smoothed her hair back with careful fingers, undoing tangles as if untying knots from a net that had dragged her out of dark water. Sometimes he simply held her hand and watched her breathe, eyes returning to her face again and again as though afraid that, with one blink too long, she would slip beyond sight.

In the blue hours, those seam-thin minutes before dawn, she practiced what the other world had taught her to hear. Inhale: weight, pain, the tug of IV tape against skin. Exhale: a hinge, a hush, the faintest thinning of the veil. She did not push. She waited at the threshold and counted her heartbeats like beads—one, two, three, listening for the soft knocks she'd been warned about. Nothing came. Still she waited, learning the patience of tides.

Emma visited on Fridays with warmth and a contraband muffin that made the nurses pretend to scowl. She brought office gossip soft as cotton and laughter that remembered not to be loud. "You're stronger," Emma would say, and Ivy would find, to her surprise, that it was true. Strength did not announce itself; it accrued, the way light gathers on water.

Tests, scans, numbers, days wore their hospital names and moved on. Ivy learned the corridor's map by the squeak of the cart wheels and the rhythm of nurses' steps. She learned her own body again, the reach that didn't shake, the stand that didn't sway, the walk that made the monitor keep its tempo. Each victory was small and, therefore, enormous.

When fear woke her, sudden, ice-cold, certain she had dreamed her way into a world where her father could not find her, she would turn her head and find Liam there, half-asleep in the chair, his fingers still threaded through hers. His thumb would stir, tracing a quiet reassurance along her knuckle. "I'm here," he'd murmur without opening his eyes, and the words would steady the room.

The ache for her father did not diminish; it refined. The memory of Ethan's outstretched arm did not fade; it focused. Between one breath and the next, Ivy made her vow again, clearer now, sharper than the pain: she would learn to make her body a dock and her soul the sea. She would find the hinge in darkness, and when the true door opened, she would know it by the way the world went quiet and the light remembered her name.

Ivy's body was a map of damage, bones set and braced, organs bruised, lacerations stitched in neat, relentless lines, but the fiercest battle raged inside her. Regaining strength became a singular creed. Each measured breath, each faltering step down the corridor was a vow carved in quiet: she would find the answers; she would find Ethan; she would reclaim what was taken. Her mission was simple and absolute. Get well, prepare.

Day by day, she pushed farther. Her resolve burned brighter than the ache that shadowed her movements. The fog of exhaustion thinned as purpose hardened into shape. She had a goal now, one that consumed every waking thought: heal. Learn. Return. She would study yoga, not as exercise but as the ancient craft Ethan had hinted at, breath as key, stillness as door, attention as the hinge and she would unlock the passage back to her father. Nothing else mattered.

Doctors noted the change without being able to name it. Charts improved, but there was something beyond charts: a heat in her gaze, a steadiness in her hands, the way her posture reclaimed its line as if a wire had been drawn taut inside her. The hollow sadness that had dimmed her spirit gave way to a fierce, quiet light. Each morning, she sat a little straighter. Each afternoon, she walked a little farther. Each evening, when fatigue dragged at her edges, she surprised it with a small, unshakable smile.

And beneath every motion, the private practice continued: breath in, weight returns; breath out, a thin hush opens. She did not force it. She waited at the seam and polished her will against its silence. Healing, preparation, purpose, three knocks she carried in her chest, until even the fluorescent room seemed to listen when she breathed.

Liam noticed it first. He watched her with cautious joy, the worry lines that had been carved into his face slowly easing. He'd braced for the worst, for a flicker that might go out, but what he saw instead was Ivy reborn: steadier eyes, a spine that seemed to remember its strength, a light that hadn't been there before the dark.

One evening, when the sun spilled a generous gold across the room and turned the IV line into a thread of fire, Liam laughed softly and shook his head in wonder. "You're so good, so happy after the accident," he said, his voice low with affection. "I think this whole thing made you realize how lucky you are in this life."

Ivy's smile was small and real. Her gaze drifted past him to the window, to the widening sky and beyond, to the unseen place where her father waited. She tightened her fingers around Liam's, letting his warmth anchor her. "Maybe," she murmured. "Or maybe it just showed me how much I have left to do."

Nearly three months later, Ivy crossed the impossible threshold.

Discharge day arrived like a sunrise after a very long night. Paperwork rustled; bracelets were snipped; the tape across her skin lifted with small, stinging goodbyes. The corridor smelled of coffee and antiseptic and victory. Nurses who had learned not to hope too loudly paused at her door with bouquets of smiles, and doctors, seasoned veterans of tragedy and triumph, traded glances over clipped charts and closed doors. She had come in a ruin of bone and bruised organ, a lattice of stitches mapping what had been torn. And yet, faster than their math allowed, she had knitted herself together. She had not complained. She had not once asked *why me*. It was as if an invisible current had taken hold of her and pulled her toward shore.

They wheeled her out only because rules demanded it. Ivy sat tall, not defiant but luminous, her hands folded in her lap with the quiet authority of someone who had learned the language of pain and refused to speak it anymore. The elevator chimed like a bell. Floors gave way to the lobby, the lobby to glass, and beyond the glass the world waited, wide, bright, loud with ordinary life. Sunlight spilled across the polished floor in a golden path that looked suspiciously like a benediction.

Liam stood at her side the way he had stood at her bedside: constant, steady, eyes never straying far from her face as though one blink too long might erase her. Pride swelled his chest until he almost had to laugh with the relief of it. She wasn't only alive; she was vibrant, burning with a purpose that made the hard lines of worry ease from his brow. He had never left. Now he watched the impossible made visible: Ivy rising where no one had expected more than survival, a kind of fire lighting her from within.

At the doors, the wheelchair brake clicked. Ivy placed her palm against the bar and stood, slowly, surely, feet finding the ground as if introducing themselves to it again. The glass parted. Outside, the air met her like a cool hand on a fevered brow. Traffic murmured. A sparrow scolded from a lamppost. The whole world seemed to inhale with her.

She looked up into the wide, bright sky, and farther, to the unseen place where her father waited, and then down to Liam's hand, open to her like a promise. She took it. The sun warmed her face. Somewhere inside, the hinge between breaths gave the softest answer.

"I'm ready," she said.

For healing. For the work. For the path that would teach her to make her body a dock and her soul the sea and, when the true door opened, to step through and find the ones she loved, and return.

Ivy kept her secret locked tight. The world would never understand. If she spoke even a syllable about standing beside her father like a ghost, about the boy with the outstretched hand and the promise to teach her, the doctors would file it under trauma, the nurses under kindness, and the charts under delusion. So she smiled when she was supposed to smile, thanked those who needed thanking, and tucked her true purpose deeper than breath, where no stethoscope could reach.

Liam guided her wheelchair toward the bright spill of the exit. Paper bracelets snipped; signatures traded hands; a nurse pressed a final packet of instructions into Liam's palm. The doors parted with a sigh, and the outside rushed in, cool air brushing her face, carrying the faint, clean bite of autumn. Sunlight climbed her skin as if reacquainting itself with her. It felt different now, edged in meaning. Everything did.

By the car, leaning against the passenger door with a warm, easy grin, stood Officer Andrew, Liam's partner, broad-shouldered, wind-ruffled, the kind of steady presence that made sidewalks feel safer. "Welcome back, Ivy," he said, stepping forward to help. "We've missed you." His hand was careful on the chair's handle; his eyes, unguardedly kind.

They eased her to standing by the open door—the hospital's final rule satisfied, the world's first one reinstated: gravity. Tires ticked on the gravel; a gull called somewhere above the roofline; life moved around them as if the last three months had been a held breath released.

Ivy looked past the parking lot to the wide, clean sky, and farther—toward the unseen place where a promise waited at the edge of light. She smoothed her palm over the car's cool frame and met Liam's gaze. A private vow pulsed in the quiet between them: heal, learn, return. She settled into the seat, the belt clicked home, and the door drew the moment closed with a soft, decisive thud.

The engine turned over. The sun laid a bright path on the windshield. The next chapter of her journey did not announce itself with trumpets. It opened like a hinge, quiet, sure, as the car rolled forward and Ivy carried her secret into the day.

Liam stayed faithfully by her side, his quiet strength a constant comfort. He cooked, he cleaned, he filled the apartment with the small mercies of ordinary care, fresh sheets, warm soup, a lamp clicked on before dusk, slipping away only when the precinct called him back like a tide. Ivy never told him what truly weighed on her soul. She let his steadiness hold the edges of her days while the center of her longing remained hidden, tender as a burn.

In the rare hours when she was alone, the rooms changed temperature. Silence gathered in the corners, dense and listening. Ivy wandered slowly through that hush, fingertips gliding over chair backs and picture frames, the lip of a mug, as though touch might conjure what sight could not. Her voice, when it came, was barely more than breath, a secret offered to the air.

At the window, where sunlight poured like golden silk and dust motes drifted like quiet planets, she tipped her face to the sky and let the ache rise unguarded. "Dad…" she murmured, the word soft and breaking at once. "I miss you. I miss you so much." Tears brimmed and slid, warm against the cool of her cheek.

"I promise I will find a way to see you again," she whispered, fingers pressing to the glass as though the world could be thinner with help. "There has to be a way. Please… please help me. Show me how to find Ethan. I know he's the key. He can help me, I feel it. Just give me a sign, anything…"

The room held still. Far below, a siren sighed and faded. Ivy closed her eyes and listened for the seam between breaths, the hush that might one day open like a hinge. She did not push. She simply stood in the gold and the quiet, vow bright in her chest, waiting for the faintest answer to tremble the air.

The wind stirred faintly against the glass, almost as if answering. Ivy closed her eyes, folded her arms around herself, and held fast to the thin, shining thread of hope that had pulled her out of the dark. She would not give up. Not now. Not ever.

She built her days into a scaffold: morning exercises to coax strength back into muscle and bone; breathwork at noon to steady the mind; a measured walk each afternoon to teach her legs the old language of distance. Emma came twice a week, mat under one arm, that warm, unstoppable smile under the other and guided Ivy through slow, deliberate sequences. "Breathe here," Emma would murmur, palm hovering a respectful inch from Ivy's back. "Lengthen. Soften. Stay." Support and encouragement braided into discipline; each pose became a promise kept.

Ivy worked without theatrics and without mercy. The relentlessness of it filled Liam with a quiet pride that he carried like a secret medal. He watched her chart the small victories on the calendar: a steadier balance today, an easier rise from the chair tomorrow. He learned to hear the difference in her breath—when fatigue asked to stop and when resolve said not yet.

The walk lengthened. One block, then two. Four. The corner store is to the corner after that. She timed nothing and measured everything: the feel of the pavement under her shoes, the way her stride found its rhythm, the lightness that arrived one breath earlier each day. Within weeks, she was covering a full kilometer, marveling that her body now carried her farther in the same space of time. Pace had returned like a friend who knew the door code.

Each evening, she stood again by the window, sweat cooling on her skin, the city exhaling around her. She pressed her palm to the glass, felt the wind answer, and in the quiet seam between breaths renewed the vow that had become her spine: heal, learn, return.

In the morning, the rich, inviting aroma of fresh coffee pulled Liam upright before his eyes were fully open. He swung his legs out of bed and hurried to the kitchen, where the table was already set, mugs steaming, toast stacked, fruit gleaming in a glass bowl.

Ivy stood there, elegantly dressed, her lustrous dark hair swept back in a sleek, polished style, makeup immaculate, and a radiant, captivating smile lighting her face like sunrise.

Liam stopped in the doorway, astonished. "What's going on? Why are you dressed up so early?"

"I'm going back to work, starting today," Ivy said, warmth in her smile as she handed him a cup.

He returned it, half grin, half disbelief. "When did you decide that? And why didn't you tell me before?"

She crossed to him, kissed him softly, and brushed her thumb along his jaw. "I spoke with Vincent yesterday. He said I could return whenever I felt ready. I told him I'd start tomorrow, which, as it turns out, is today."

Liam tilted his head, studying her with affectionate curiosity. "Why didn't you call me, or say anything last night?"

Her dazzling smile flashed again. "You got home so late, and I promised myself I'd never call when you're on duty. What if you were hiding somewhere to protect yourself, and your phone started ringing because of me? I won't take that risk."

Liam chuckled, shaking his head. "You've been watching too many spy movies. I keep telling you, I don't do that kind of work."

Ivy grinned, adjusting the delicate bracelet Liam had given her, light skating over the tiny charms as if approving her return. "Maybe not, but I'm not taking any chances. Besides, it's my first day back. I wanted to surprise you."

He stepped closer, brushed a loose strand from her cheek. "You've already surprised me, in the best way. I'm proud of you, Ivy."

Her eyes held his, clear and unwavering. "I'm ready, Liam. I can't let what happened define me forever. It's time I take back my life."

"I know you will," he said, the certainty in his voice as warm as his hand at the small of her back. "You've already come so far."

Cutlery chimed; the coffee maker sighed its last breath. Ivy slipped the strap of her purse over her shoulder and checked her reflection once more, sleek hair, steady gaze, the bracelet's shy glimmer at her wrist. The woman in the glass looked like someone who had walked through fire and learned the language of light.

"Let me drive you," Liam said.

She hesitated only a heartbeat, then nodded, "Okay."

The morning air met them cool and clean. On the way down, the elevator mirrored them in panels of brushed steel: his broad, watchful presence beside her poised stillness. In the car, they let the city's soft roar fill the quiet. At red lights, he glanced over, as if reminding himself she was truly there; at green, she watched the sunlight braid across the windshield and felt her breath even out to its old, dependable rhythm.

Outside her building, Liam pulled to the curb. He rounded to her side, opened the door, and offered his hand like a promise. She took it, stepped onto the sidewalk, and for a second simply stood, letting the familiar façade resolve into meaning, the glass, the brass, the revolving door turning an ordinary morning into a threshold.

"You want me to walk you in?" he asked.

She smiled. "I've got it." Then, softer: "Thank you."

He leaned in, kissed her temple. "Text me if you need anything."

"I will." She meant it.

Inside, the lobby air was cool and scented faintly with citrus and copy paper. Heads turned. The receptionist's face broke into a grin; someone near the elevators whispered her name with relief stitched into it. When the doors slid open on her floor, applause started, soft, spontaneous, quickly swallowed by laughter at itself. Emma was the first to reach her, folding Ivy into a careful hug that still felt like sunlight.

"You look incredible," Emma said, eyes bright. "You sure you're ready?"

Ivy's smile tilted, steady. "I'm sure."

Vincent appeared behind them, a file tucked to his side like a shield. "Good to have you back," he said with a rare, unguarded warmth. "Only when you feel up to speed, easing in is fine. Your office is exactly as you left it."

"Thank you," Ivy said, and meant more than the words could carry.

Her office waited—glass wall, familiar desk, the chair that once felt too big and now felt exactly right. A vase of white lilies glowed on the credenza, the card unsigned. She set her purse down, touched the bracelet with a thumb, and sat. The screen woke to life; the old password still knew her. Emails stacked like waves. She answered the first one, then the second, fingers moving with a quiet authority that surprised her.

When the hum of the floor settled, she leaned back and closed her eyes for a breath. Inhale: weight, the ordinary texture of the day. Exhale: a seam, fine as silk. She didn't push. She stood at that inner threshold and listened. Nothing opened, but the listening itself steadied her, a small anchor dropped into deep water.

A soft knock at the door, this one made of wood and habit. Emma peered in, wiggling a brow. "Lunch later? And I found a class you might actually like. Breath-focused. Minimal pretzel shapes."

Ivy smiled. "Perfect. Text me the details."

Emma's grin widened. "Welcome back, boss." She vanished, leaving the door ajar just enough to let life in.

Ivy turned to the window. The city breathed below. Somewhere beyond its scaffolds and sky, a boundary waited, patient as the tide. She touched the bracelet, cool metal, warm memory and felt the vow glide back into place: heal, learn, return. Then she faced the screen, shoulders squared, and began—work first, breath steady, the hinge inside her quiet and sure as she stepped fully, deliberately, into the next part of her life.

The phone rang; she answered on the first chime. Her lips curved. "I'll be right there."

The elevator's sleek doors parted to a chorus of surprised smiles and warm voices. "Ivy! Welcome back!" someone called as she stepped in.

"Thank you," she replied, gracious and composed, though her heart beat a shade quicker. At the executive floor, the doors slid open again, and she moved with quiet confidence down the corridor toward Vincent's office. The heavy door stood slightly ajar. Vincent—tall, impeccably tailored, carrying that rare blend of command and kindness—looked up and broke into a broad smile.

"Ivy," he said, rising with an outstretched hand. "It's good to have you back."

She met his grip, firm and sure. "It's good to be back, Vincent."

He gestured to the chair opposite. "We've all missed your presence. I'll bring you up to speed on the current projects. I'm just glad to see you healthy and ready."

"I'm ready for whatever comes," she said, voice calm, eyes steady.

"That's the Ivy I know." He nodded, approval clean and unforced.

They got to it. As Vincent briefed and Ivy listened, asked, answered, the old cadence returned, notes turning into music. With each exchange, her confidence rose, not as a surge but as a tide, lifting everything it touched. The past stepped back. The future leaned in.

Vincent, meticulous to the bone, slid a folder across the desk with the care of a chess player placing a decisive piece. "Ivy, I have a persistent client. I want you to handle his order. He's opening a new office just outside Toronto and wants the building to be one of a kind. I've told him you're back. All the details are in here."

His gaze held hers, intent. "If you need anything, come to me directly. This client is a big deal, very expensive taste, and I want you to remain as exceptional as ever."

Ivy laid her palm on the folder, felt its weight, and smiled, quiet, assured. "Consider it done," she said, and the words sounded exactly like a door opening.

The hours thinned and slid past as Ivy immersed herself in reports, project updates, and client files. Being back felt faintly unreal, like stepping into a scene she knew by heart, yet it steadied her. Colleagues drifted by in waves: a few quick hellos at the door, others lingering, grateful to say how much they'd missed her quiet judgment and unflappable calm.

By mid-afternoon, she leaned back, stretched, and rolled the tension from her shoulders. Her phone buzzed.

Unknown Number: *Welcome back, Ivy. I see you made it in.*

A cool thread of dread moved down her spine. She glanced across the open floor. Nothing was out of place. The soft murmur of voices, the clipped rhythm of keyboards, the steady wash of the HVAC, ordinary, almost soothing. Her fingers hovered above the screen. Then she locked the phone and slid it into her drawer, the decision neat and final.

She stood, smoothed her jacket, and walked to the conference room. Vincent was already there with a cluster of high-profile clients. Ivy paused at the threshold, gathered herself, and stepped inside, professional composure settling over her like a well-fitted coat.

The meeting opened without friction, slides advancing, figures aligning, questions dispatched with practiced ease. Halfway through, a powerful investor with a reputation for being difficult pivoted toward Ivy.

"I've heard a lot about you," he said, cool as glass. "I hope your… recent situation won't affect your ability to deliver."

The air thinned. Pens stilled, chairs ceased their small adjustments. Every gaze found Ivy.

She met his eyes and didn't look away. When she spoke, her voice was even, steady, measured to reach every corner of the room. "My commitment and capabilities have never changed, nor will they."

A fractional lift of his eyebrow. The faintest suggestion of respect, or calculation. "We'll see."

Vincent caught up with her in the hallway, matching her pace. "You handled that perfectly. Not everyone would've stayed that composed."

Ivy allowed the smallest curve of a smile. "I've been through worse."

Back at her office, her phone buzzed.

Unknown Number: I'll see, indeed…

Her pulse kicked once, hard, but her expression stayed cool, unmarked. Whoever this was had chosen the wrong person to intimidate, she read the message again, let the spike of adrenaline burn off, then set the phone face down and drew a slow, measured breath.

Not today. I won't let this ruin my first day back.

A soft knock cut through her thoughts. The door edged open and Emma, her closest friend at work, all warmth and ballast, peeked in with a bright, familiar smile.

"I hear you're back and already stirring up the boardroom," she teased as she stepped inside.

Ivy's serious expression eased. "It's so good to see you, Em." They shared a brief hug.

Emma leaned back to study her. "You look amazing… but there's that look in your eyes. You're tense."

Ivy exhaled, a small shake of her head. "It's just… everything. Walking back in, the pressure, and—," she paused, the corner of her mouth tightening, "—a little weirdness I don't want to give oxygen to right now."

Emma tipped her head, reading her the way only Emma could. "You've been through enough. You need a reset. Let's do something after work."

A faint smile unspooled across Ivy's face as the answer arrived. "Actually, yes. Come to yoga with me tonight? You're always telling me to slow down and breathe. I think I finally need that."

Emma's grin lit the room. "Finally! I've been trying to get you to come for ages. I'll pick you up. Trust me, you'll love it."

Ivy's chuckle came easy this time, the weight on her shoulders easing a notch. "Deal. It's a date."

As Emma left, Ivy's gaze drifted to her phone. Another message pulsed on the screen: *Good decision, you are on the right track.* A brief furrow touched her brow. She locked the device and slid it into her purse, the motion deliberate. Whoever was behind the messages would not script her day. Tonight was for peace, for friendship, for finding her center again.

The yoga studio was a quiet oasis tucked between hard-breathing streets. Warm, amber light pooled across the polished floor; soft instrumental music threaded through the air; a faint ribbon of lavender greeted them at the door. Ivy and Emma stepped inside, shoes whispering against the entry mat, the low murmur of voices, and the hush of breath settling around them like calm.

They unrolled their mats side by side in the wide, breath-quiet room. The instructor, a graceful woman named Alina, moved like a hush through the rows, adjusting shoulders, lengthening spines, offering guidance in a voice that felt like warm water. Wisdom and serenity seemed to settle around her like a shawl. The moment her eyes met Ivy's, she started toward them.

"Hi," Alina said, smiling. "I'm so happy you could make it. I'm glad I finally got to meet you in person."

Ivy and Emma traded a quick, baffled glance.

"Alina! You saw her once before, when she came with me, remember?" Emma said.

Alina's smile tilted, a faint acknowledgment. "Yes, of course I remember. But that was before her friend told me about her."

Ivy frowned lightly. "Which friend are you talking about?"

"Your friend is named Ethan," Alina said.

Ivy's gaze swept the room, urgency edging her voice. "Is he here? Is he coming for yoga, too?"

Alina's gentleness didn't waver. "Honey, he can never come here. But I know him."

Without another word, Alina turned and glided to the front of the room, hands at her heart center, and the studio settled into a hush.

The class moved through quiet arcs and measured breaths, gentle folds, lengthening spines, the kind of stillness that loosens what the day knots tight. With each slow inhale, Ivy felt the static of the afternoon ebb; with each exhale, the weight of it slipped further away. By the time they reached the final rest, *Savasana*, Corpse Pose, she lay unmoving, as if suspended in warm water, her body feather-light, her mind surprisingly clear.

When it ended, students rose softly and drifted out, voices low, mats whispering against the floor. Ivy lingered. She crossed to Alina, who greeted her with a warm, knowing smile.

"Alina," Ivy said, voice pitched just above a whisper, "may I ask you something… unusual?"

"Of course," Alina replied, calm as a still pool.

Ivy glanced around, then lowered her voice another shade. "I've read things. Heard stories. Is it true that some people can separate their souls from their bodies and exist outside themselves for a while?"

Alina regarded her for a quiet moment, then inclined her head. "Across many ancient traditions and spiritual disciplines, what you describe is known as astral projection, an out-of-body experience. With sustained meditation, or in certain altered states, the soul is said to travel beyond the physical form."

Ivy's eyes widened. "So it is not just a myth?"

Alina's serene smile deepened. "For those who have experienced it, it is as real as breath. But it is not a pursuit to take lightly. It demands years of discipline, equilibrium, and a rigorous understanding of both the physical and the spiritual."

Alina tilted her head, studying Ivy. "Why do you ask? You've already touched it. For you, returning to that place will be easier."

Ivy hesitated, a faint smile flickering as she tried to deflect. "Just… curiosity. And how do you know so much about me?"

Alina's gaze softened. "Curiosity often leads us to the answers we need, when we're ready. And as I told you before, Ethan is my friend as well."

Ivy's expression stilled. "May I have his address or phone number, please? I need to speak with him. It's very important. Please…"

Alina's smile remained gentle. "Honey, I don't know where he lives, and I don't have his number. I only see him once in a while."

Ivy nodded her thanks and returned to Emma, mind racing. She wasn't sure she believed it, or that any of it explained what had been stirring at the edges of her days, but something deeper insisted that a threshold had just been crossed, and a larger mystery waited beyond the door she had opened.

Weeks slipped past, and Ivy gave herself to the practice with quiet ferocity. Morning and evening, she moved, did breath work, balanced, and performed long-held stretches that found the edges of her strength and pressed a little farther. Alina noticed the change and, without prying, nourished it with gentle corrections and steady encouragement, unaware of the deeper purpose Ivy carried beneath her composure.

Emma, steadfast as ever, joined whenever she could. "You're turning into a yoga warrior," she teased one evening as they rolled up their mats. "You're even better than me now."

Ivy's smile was small and sincere. "I have a reason to be."

She spoke rarely of what drove her. But late one night, after another long session, she finally broke the silence. They sat cross-legged on the floor of Ivy's apartment, candlelight fluttering against the walls, the city hushed beyond the glass. Ivy's fingers worried the edge of her mat; she drew a slow breath, steadying herself, and lifted her gaze to Emma's.

"When I was in the coma," Ivy began, her voice distant, "I wasn't just unconscious. I was somewhere else. I saw my father. I spoke to him. He wasn't alone; there was another spirit with him, a man named Ethan. I don't know how I knew his name, but I did."

Emma listened without a word, her usual playfulness replaced by a steady, quiet empathy.

"It felt more real than this world," Ivy whispered. "When I woke up, I thought I'd lost them for good. Then the messages started, the strange ones. 'I see you made it in.' 'I'll see, indeed…' I think it's Ethan. No, I know it's him."

Emma blinked. "You believe he's trying to reach you… from the other side?"

"I don't *believe*," Ivy said, her voice settling into something calm and certain. "I know. He isn't dead, he's very much alive." Hope brightened her features. After a beat, she went on, "And I believe that if I can strengthen the connection between my spirit and my body, I might be able to cross over again, just long enough to see my father… and Ethan."

Emma reached across and closed her hand over Ivy's. "Then I'm with you. I don't care how crazy it sounds. You're not doing this alone."

The next day, Ivy pushed harder. Yoga stopped being merely physical and became a bridge, breath to breath, pose to pose, a deliberate crossing. At night, she practiced under the moon, hunting a silence deep enough to feel the faint tug of that other realm.

In the days that followed, her focus sharpened. The work turned disciplined, then meditative. Emma stayed close, steady, present, though the larger truth Ivy hinted at remained just out of her reach.

One evening, after an especially intense session, Ivy's phone buzzed.

Unknown Number: You're almost there. Don't be afraid.

Her pulse quickened. She drew a slow breath and, for the first time, typed a reply.

Ivy: Who are you? Why are you watching me?

The reply arrived almost at once.

Unknown Number: You already know. We met in the middle. I was with your father. He gave me everything I needed to find you. I'm watching you, Ivy, and I can't wait to see you here again.

A second message followed on its heels.

Unknown Number: Of course… see you here, and alive.

A fine tremor moved through her hands. Across the room, Emma, mid-pour, caught the change in Ivy's face and set the cups down.

"Ivy?"

She turned slowly, voice low but sure. "It's him. It's Ethan."

Emma crossed to her. "The spirit?"

Ivy shook her head, the realization settling with a strange, luminous weight. "No. He's alive. He was with my father, but he isn't a ghost. He's living somewhere. And somehow…" She drew a breath, the words finding their shape. "He can separate his soul from his body, like astral projection."

Emma's eyes widened. "So you weren't hallucinating in the coma."

"I knew it wasn't a dream." Ivy exhaled slowly. "My father trusted Ethan. He told him about me. Ethan's been guiding me from the beginning."

That night, after Emma left, Ivy sat alone with her phone resting beside her yoga mat. The room was quiet enough to hear her own breath. The screen lit.

Ethan: You're almost ready, Ivy. When the time comes, I will help you. You must be strong. You must trust me.

Her pulse quickened, not from fear, but anticipation. For the first time, she knew she wasn't alone in this. Someone was out there. Someone who had crossed between worlds and returned. Someone her father trusted.

Ivy curled her hands into fists, heat gathering beneath her sternum. "I'm coming, Dad," she breathed. "And Ethan, whoever you are, I'll be ready."

The next day, she told Emma everything, end to end: the coma; the impossible clarity of her father's spirit with a man named Ethan beside him; the messages that had followed like footprints across her days. Emma listened without a flicker of doubt, only a tightening resolve.

"Then we train," she said, voice low and certain. "Whatever it takes to get you there, I'm with you."

As Ivy pushed further into her meditations and spiritual training, a new chapter had quietly begun: Ethan watching from afar, preparing for the moment when their paths would cross again, not between life and death, but face-to-face in the living world.

Ethan stood still under the pale light of the moon, his physical body safely resting miles away in a secluded cabin deep within the forest. His spirit, weightless and silent, hovered unseen in the quiet darkness just outside Ivy's apartment window.

He watched over her, not as an intruder, but as a silent guardian, bound by an unbreakable promise to Cyrus. Long ago, Ethan had mastered the art of separating his soul from his body, navigating the unseen through the ancient path of astral projection, which few had ever dared to attempt. His rare ability had made him both a guardian and an outsider.

The night Ivy slipped deeper into her meditations, Ethan's spirit lingered nearby. He observed her steady progress, the way her breath slowed, her heartbeat softened, her spirit stretching ever so slightly toward the veil. He knew the signs. She was close.

From his place in the spectral plane, Ethan whispered softly, knowing his voice would only reach her subconscious, *"You're stronger than you think, Ivy. Soon… soon you'll find the doorway."* Inside, Ivy stirred faintly in her meditative state, her breath catching for a heartbeat. A faint warmth spread over her, as if someone had brushed invisible fingers across her skin.

The next morning, Ivy sat at her small kitchen table with Emma, her tea growing cold as she stared out the window thoughtfully. "Emma," she said finally, "I keep feeling like someone's near me when I meditate. Not in a bad way… like they're watching, protecting me." Emma wrapped her hands around her mug. "Ethan?" Ivy nodded slowly. "It has to be. It's the only thing that makes sense. He said he'd help me when I was ready. What if he's watching so he knows the exact moment to guide me?" Emma's eyes widened. "You mean… his spirit is already here?"

"I believe it is," Ivy whispered. "And I believe I'm getting close." That night, Ivy prepared for her most intense meditation yet. Emma stayed with her, sitting quietly nearby as Ivy settled onto her mat. Ethan's spirit waited just beyond the veil, watching as Ivy's breathing slowed, her body relaxed, and her energy began to expand outward. He saw the faint shimmer of her soul stir inside her physical form. *"Not yet,"* he whispered, restraining himself from intervening too soon. *"You're almost ready, Ivy. The first crossing must be yours alone."*

Ivy's mind brushed faintly against the edges of the unknown, a soft pulse of energy meeting the barrier between the living world and the spirit realm. Startled, she gasped and fell back, her eyes snapping open. Emma rushed to her side. "Are you okay?" Ivy nodded, her heart racing. "I touched something. I felt it. It was real."

Far away, Ethan opened his eyes in his forest refuge, a faint smile crossing his face. The time was near. Soon, he would no longer have to watch from afar. Soon, he and Ivy would meet again, in both spirit and reality.

CHAPTER THREE – The Threshold Between Worlds

The room was silent except for the gentle flicker of candle flames and the soft rhythm of Ivy's breathing. The air felt heavier tonight, charged with something unseen yet undeniable. Ivy sat cross-legged on her mat, her posture perfectly still, her eyes closed in deep focus.

Emma sat a short distance away, watching with anxious reverence. They had prepared for this night for weeks. Ivy had pushed her body and mind to the edge of discipline, and tonight everything felt aligned.

Ivy's breath slowed to an almost imperceptible whisper. She mentally followed the flow of energy through her body, visualizing light traveling through her veins, surrounding her heart, filling her mind. She felt weightless. The pull came stronger this time, a subtle, insistent current beckoning her beyond the boundaries of flesh and bone.

Suddenly, with a sensation like slipping through silk, Ivy felt herself detach. Her body remained grounded, but her awareness drifted upward and outward. The room below seemed distant, veiled in a hazy silver glow. She glanced down and gasped softly. There she was sitting motionless on the mat, her face serene. She had done it.

Euphoria mixed with disbelief flooded her. She floated gracefully, the walls of the apartment seeming fluid and surreal. Then, from the far corner of the room, a figure emerged from the shadows of the spirit plane.

Tall, lean, and cloaked in a faint blue luminescence, Ethan stepped forward. His eyes held the depth of countless journeys between worlds, but they softened at the sight of her. "Ivy," Ethan spoke, his voice both distant and familiar, echoing across the unseen expanse, "you've crossed the threshold."

Ivy turned to face him fully. "Ethan," she breathed. "You're real. You're alive."

He nodded solemnly. "I am. I've waited for you to reach this moment. Your father trusted me to guide you when you were ready."

Tears prickled in Ivy's eyes, but they didn't fall. "Can I see him? Is he here?" Ethan's expression softened. "Not yet. Your spirit is still learning. The connection is fragile. If you go too far, you may not return. But you've taken the first step, and that changes everything."

Ivy hovered in stunned silence, her breath caught between disbelief and awakening. "This feels like a dream… but it's not, is it?" she whispered. "Why can I do this? How is any of this even possible? And the real question is, why now? Why did it finally work?"

"Because you're meant to," Ethan said gently. "And there's more at stake than you know." The faint pull of her body began to tug at her spirit. Ethan sensed it and stepped closer. "We're out of time for now. You must return. But I will find you again, in both worlds. You're not alone in this, Ivy."

With a soft shimmer, the world began to blur around her. Ivy felt herself spiraling downward, back through layers of light and shadow. She gasped awake, her chest rising sharply as Emma rushed to her side. "Ivy!" Emma cried. "What happened?"

Ivy smiled through the tears in her eyes. "I did it. I crossed over. I saw him. I spoke to Ethan."

Emma stared in wonder. "What did he say?" Ivy's gaze hardened with new purpose. "That this is only the beginning."

The next evening, Ivy sat in meditation again, determined to strengthen the fragile connection. Emma sat nearby as always, pretending to scroll through her phone but sneaking glances at her friend with a mixture of awe and nervousness.

As Ivy's spirit slipped free once more, the world shifted to its ethereal form: soft silver hues, the flicker of candlelight transformed into radiant orbs. Ethan was already waiting, leaning casually against a shimmering column of light. "You're getting better at this," he remarked warmly as Ivy approached.

Ivy smiled. "I had a good teacher, even if he prefers to stay mysterious."

Ethan's eyes twinkled with amusement, then drifted toward the soft glow where Emma's silhouette could faintly be seen, tethered to the living world. He tilted his head thoughtfully. "I have to say, your friend Emma… she's got a spark. Loyal, fearless, funny… and did you notice she talks to herself when you meditate? Adorable."

Ivy chuckled softly, crossing her arms. "You're watching Emma now?" Ethan gave a playful shrug. "Hard not to. If I were alive and walking your world, I might even ask her out. Shame I'm technically incorporeal most of the time."

Before Ivy could respond, a soft ripple cut through the stillness, a new presence emerged: graceful, calm, and radiant. Both Ivy and Ethan turned in astonishment as the yoga instructor's Alina luminous spirit form stepped into view.

Ethan straightened, visibly surprised. "Well… this is unexpected." Alina smiled gently. "I sensed someone had been lingering in my class energies. I followed the trail here. You must be the watcher." Ethan laughed quietly and bowed with a mock flourish. "Guilty. Ethan. I specialize in… well, complicated cases."

Alina extended a graceful hand. "I'm Alina. I teach souls how to listen, even when they don't know they're searching." They shook hands, energy swirling softly around them. Ivy watched the exchange with curiosity and relief. "You two know each other now?" she asked.

Alina gave a knowing nod. "Not until this moment. But we've traveled similar paths. I've crossed over a few times myself, though never as boldly as you, Ivy." Ethan glanced at Ivy, then back to Alina. "Looks like we've both been looking out for the same person."

A rare warmth passed between the two spirit guides. Ivy smiled at the unexpected alliance forming before her. "I feel safer already," she said, her tone light but sincere.

Ethan chuckled, giving Alina a sideways glance. "I have a feeling I'll be bumping into you a lot more now."

Alina's soft laughter echoed across the veil. "I wouldn't mind."

The three stood in a rare moment of calm at the crossroads between two worlds, unaware that their bond would soon be tested by darker forces that stirred beyond the veil. The days settled into a rhythm. Ivy and Emma returned to the familiar routine of office life, client meetings, project deadlines, and coffee breaks filled with whispered jokes. Ivy felt stronger, more alive than ever, carrying her secret purpose quietly beneath the surface.

After work, they went to yoga as always. Alina, calm and poised, guided them through the sequences, but now Ivy understood the subtle depth behind her instructions. A silent glance from Alina would sometimes hold an extra layer of meaning, an unspoken acknowledgment of what lay beyond the physical poses.

One evening, after Emma left and the studio was quiet, Ivy slipped into meditation. Her spirit separated easily now, flowing into the luminous plane where Ethan waited, his form shimmering warmly. Alina appeared beside him moments later, graceful as always. Ethan smiled at Ivy, his tone playful as usual. "You're becoming a pro at this."

"I've had good help," Ivy replied warmly. Then she grew thoughtful. "I've been thinking... could we *go* somewhere? Visit another place while I'm like this?"

Ethan and Alina exchanged a quick look, their shared energy silently agreeing. Ethan gestured to the glowing horizon. "Anywhere you want. The spirit plane touches every part of creation. Where do you want to go?"

Ivy didn't hesitate. "I've always dreamed of seeing the moon up close."

Ethan chuckled, and Alina smiled softly. "A good choice."

With a thought, the three of them surged upward, breaking through the veil. Stars blurred past as they soared weightlessly into space, the radiant blue Earth shrinking behind them. The moon loomed ahead, massive and cold, its pale gray surface covered in soft dust and jagged craters.

They drifted down to the surface, the silence profound and awe-inspiring. Ivy stood breathless, her spirit form lightly touching the gray dust. The Earth hung in the black sky like a glowing sapphire. "It's beautiful," Ivy whispered. "I never imagined it like this."

Ethan nodded. "Few get to see it from here."

As they explored, Alina suddenly paused, sensing something. Ethan followed her gaze. Across the vast darkness of the moon's shadowed far side, an outline began to materialize. They approached cautiously. Ivy's breath caught as she saw what lay before them: an enormous alien city, half-buried under the lunar surface. Towering spires of obsidian-like metal rose into the darkness, flickering faintly with eerie blue lights. Smooth, geometric structures spiraled downward into the ground as if the city extended miles below the surface. The city was silent, but alive with energy. "What is this place?" Ivy whispered.

Ethan's voice was low, almost reverent. "A hidden civilization. One of many. Some say they've always been here, long before humans even existed." Ivy stepped closer to the edge of a vast subterranean entrance. Strange, fluid symbols glowed along the walls.

"Do they know we're here?" Ivy asked.

Alina whispered, "I don't think they care. We are only passing shadows to them."

As the wonder filled her, Ivy turned to Ethan, her expression softening. "I want to ask again… my father. Will I see him soon? Will I be able to spend time with him?"

Ethan looked at her, his playful side gone. "You will. You're getting stronger every day. Your father is in a safe part of the spirit realm, but the crossings are delicate. I promised him I'd guide you there when you were ready."

Tears shimmered in Ivy's eyes, suspended like stars in the weightless plane. "I miss him so much, Ethan."

Ethan gently touched her shoulder. "I know. And you will see him. But tonight, we should return. You've stretched far. It's time to rest."

They ascended silently from the hidden city, the alien towers shrinking behind them as they soared back toward Earth. The stars watched wordlessly as Ivy drifted back into her body, Emma's concerned face hovering over her.

"Ivy? Are you okay?" Ivy smiled faintly, her face aglow with exhaustion and wonder. "More than okay. I just visited the moon."

Emma blinked, utterly speechless, a rare event. "How? You were out for like… two minutes. I'm officially jealous."

Ivy chuckled softly. "It felt like a whole day over there. We walked through their city, saw how they live… It was beautiful. And Alina was with us too."

Emma froze, her eyes locked on Ivy. "Shut up. You mean *our* Alina?" Ivy nodded, her smile deepening. Emma's jaw dropped. "I *cannot* wait to grill her about this."

The weekend arrived with the warmth of early summer. Ivy and Liam had decided on something simple, something *normal* for once—a backyard barbecue at Liam's cozy house on the outskirts of the city. The scent of grilled food drifted through the air, blending with the soft sound of laughter and the clinking of glasses.

Ivy stood at the patio table, arranging plates while Emma hovered nearby, sneaking bites of potato salad. "You know, for someone who just visited the moon, you throw a pretty down-to-earth party," Emma joked. Ivy laughed. "Even spirit travelers need burgers and fresh air."

Liam appeared with a tray of perfectly grilled steaks and vegetables, setting it down with mock ceremony. "Ladies and gentlemen, I present the masterpiece." Alina, dressed casually yet still radiating her calm elegance, smiled. "It smells wonderful, Liam."

Two of Liam's friends, Alex and Jordan, both firefighters with the same effortless charm as Liam, joined the group, along with his partner, Officer Andrew. Alex raised an eyebrow when introduced to Alina. "You're the famous yoga teacher?" he asked, shaking her hand warmly. "Liam says Ivy practically lives at your studio."

Alina laughed gently. "I try to keep her grounded, even when she's reaching for the stars."

Emma gave Ivy a teasing glance. "Literally."

Liam passed around drinks as everyone settled onto the deck chairs. The sun cast a warm glow across the yard. "So," Jordan asked, leaning back, "how did you all meet? Seems like an interesting bunch." Ivy and Emma exchanged a quick glance.

Ivy answered smoothly, "Work, yoga, life. You know how paths cross."

Liam smiled at Ivy, his gaze softening. "Ivy has a way of pulling people together."

As the evening settled in, the group gathered around the soft crackle of the fire pit. Ivy leaned back, her gaze drifting toward Alina, who sat cross-legged on the edge of the bench, her expression calm, distant, like she was still halfway across the world.

"Tell us something we don't know about you," Emma nudged, half-teasing. Alina smiled, her eyes flickering with memory. "Alright. Ever heard of meditating at the edge of a live volcano?" The group went silent.

"I was in Iceland," she began, her voice smooth and soft, almost hypnotic. "I had been traveling alone for weeks, no plans, no deadlines, just following the wind. One morning, I heard from a local about a crater, still active, steaming, but calm. It wasn't on any tourist map. I hiked for hours through mist and silence until I found it: this massive, blackened mouth in the Earth, glowing faintly from within, like it held a sleeping beast."

"You didn't go near it, right?" Jordan asked, half laughing, half serious.

"Oh, I did," Alina said with a glint in her eyes.

"I sat at the very edge, where the earth trembled just enough to remind you that it was alive. I crossed my legs, closed my eyes, and let myself drift."

"You meditated there?" Alex said, incredulous. "I did for hours. And in that silence, with the heat rising from the deep and the wind howling over the ice, I felt something… ancient. Like the Earth itself was whispering secrets. I saw visions of fire and birth, destruction and renewal. And I understood something: even the most violent forces can have peace at their core."

The group was quiet for a moment, suspended in the gravity of her story. "Of course," Alina added with a chuckle, "I also got the worst sunburn of my life. Iceland's sun is sneaky." Laughter broke the spell, but Ivy's gaze lingered on her. She had the feeling Alina wasn't just telling a story, she was sharing a piece of her soul.

As the laughter from Alina's volcanic tale faded into a comfortable hush, Alex leaned forward, elbows on his knees, a crooked grin spreading across his face.

"Alright," he said, waving a hand. "Enough of mystical volcano vibes. Let me bring things back down to Earth, specifically, to an attic in Scarborough."

Jordan groaned. "Oh no. Not the cat story."

"Oh yes, the cat story," Alex said, eyes twinkling.

"So, we get a call about smoke coming from a house, turns out it was just some overenthusiastic incense. But as we're getting ready to leave, this sweet old lady begs us to help her with something else. Her cat, Mr. Picklesis trapped in the attic crawlspace."

"Mr. Pickles?" Emma chuckled.

"Yeah. Don't let the name fool you. That cat was Satan in a fur coat. So I volunteer because, you know, I'm a nice guy, and climb up there with nothing but a flashlight and misplaced confidence."

He spread his hands dramatically. "What I didn't know was that the crawlspace was barely two feet high, filled with ancient insulation, and Mr. Pickles was not trapped. He was hiding. Waiting."

The group laughed, but Alex held up a hand.

"I reach him, finally, after about fifteen minutes of slithering like a worm. I call his name. He hisses. Then, just as I reach out, he bolts. Not away, no right over my back. I flinch, bang my head on a rafter, twist around, and end up stuck. Legit stuck. Face down, legs flailing behind me like I'm trying to swim through fiberglass."

"Rescue mission turned into a rescue-for-the-rescuer," Jordan added, barely holding back his laugh. "Exactly. I had to radio it in. 'Yeah, this is Alex… I require extraction… from an attic… due to aggressive feline activity.'" Everyone burst into laughter.

Alex leaned back with a triumphant smirk. "Moral of the story? Never trust a cat named Mr. Pickles. Especially if incense is involved."

Even Alina chuckled, her calm serenity shaken by the image. Ivy wiped a tear of laughter from her cheek. "You might not have found enlightenment, but you definitely found humility."

"Among other things," Alex said, still brushing imaginary fiberglass off his sleeves.

After the room settled from another burst of laughter, all eyes shifted to Jordan, who had been quietly sipping his drink with a suspicious smile. "Don't look at me like that," he said. "I'm not topping Volcano Woman or the Cat King of Insulation. But if we're sharing stories… I've got one that still haunts my career."

"Go on," Ivy encouraged, already grinning. Jordan sighed theatrically. "Alright. Picture this, it's a heatwave, middle of July. We get a call about someone stuck in an elevator in a downtown condo. Easy, right? I've done a hundred of these. I grab my gear, feeling heroic, like a firefighter version of James Bond. I even had new sunglasses. Big mistake."

Alex smirked, "Oh, I remember this."

"Of course you do, you were the one laughing first," Jordan shot back, then continued. "So I get there. The elevator is stuck between floors. I pry open the doors just enough to peek in, and there she is. A woman, mid-thirties, dressed like she's headed to a Vogue cover shoot, holding a Chihuahua in one arm and a mango smoothie in the other."

Emma already started giggling. "She looks up at me and goes, 'Oh, thank God, I've been in here for fifteen minutes and Biscuit is traumatized.' I think she meant the dog, but I wasn't totally sure. So I lower myself in like some kind of clumsy action star, squeeze into the elevator, and tell her we're going to get her out."

"And that's when Biscuit lost it," Alex added, shaking his head. Jordan nodded solemnly. "The dog went feral. I guess my sunglasses or my scent or my *existence* offended him. He launched at me, tiny jaws of fury. I dropped the flashlight, tripped over her handbag, elbowed the smoothie into the wall, and fell flat on my back in a puddle of mango shame." The group exploded with laughter.

"She erupted into a cacophony of screams, Biscuit was emitting low growls, and I found myself reclining there, contemplating, 'This is how my legacy concludes. Not in flames. Not in triumph. But amidst fruit juice and a diminutive dog named Biscuit.'" Even Alina had to stifle her laughter with her hand.

"So, moral of the story?" Jordan said, raising his glass. "Elevators are dangerous. Smoothies are slippery. And never trust a dog small enough to fit in a purse, but mean enough to fight for one."

When the laughter finally died down, Officer Andrew cleared his throat and leaned back, arms crossed, a sly smile tugging at the corner of his mouth. "I've got one," he said in that calm, serious tone only cops and villains in old movies use. "But it's not your typical patrol story. This one's got mystery, betrayal, and… tofu."

"Tofu?" Ivy raised an eyebrow. Andrew nodded. "Let me take you back to a chilly Tuesday evening. I'm on night duty. Quiet neighborhood. I stop by a 24-hour organic market to grab a coffee. As I leave, a guy sprints out the back door, hands full, hoodie up, suspicious as hell."

Alex leaned forward. "A robbery?"

"That's what I thought," Andrew said. "So I give chase. He's fast, but I'm faster, thank you, cardio Thursdays. I corner him in an alley. I say, 'Drop the bag and put your hands where I can see them.' He panics and throws the bag… right at me."

Jordan laughed. "And inside?" Andrew raised a hand dramatically. "Tofu. Dozens of packs of organic, gluten-free, high-protein tofu. I'm staring at it like I just caught the great soy bandit of Toronto."

"He robbed the store… for tofu?" Emma said, baffled.

"Apparently," Andrew replied, deadpan. "But here's where it gets weird. As I'm calling it in, the guy starts muttering, 'They're watching. It's not tofu. It's all a cover.' I think he's nuts, right? But then the store manager shows up… and he looks *terrified*."

Everyone fell silent. "The manager pulls me aside and whispers, 'Officer, we're not supposed to talk about the tofu.' I'm thinking, okay, either this is some underground soy conspiracy, or I accidentally stepped into a bad spy movie."

Alina raised an eyebrow, clearly intrigued. "So I investigate. Turns out, the guy was an ex-employee who thought the store was using tofu shipments to smuggle… something. He never found out what. Neither did I. But when I asked for the security footage the next day, the store had already 'lost' it. Gone. Poof."

"Are you serious?" Ivy asked, eyes wide.

"As serious as a tofu heist," Andrew said with a grin. "I never solved the case. Every time I drive past that place now, I swear I see someone peeking through the freezer aisle blinds."

"So… what's the moral?" Alex smirked. Andrew looked around the group. "Always trust your instincts. And never, ever underestimate tofu."

The group was still chuckling over the Great Tofu Conspiracy when all eyes turned to Emma. She raised her hands defensively. "No way. I don't have any secret tofu missions or volcano meditations. I'm just a yoga instructor, not an undercover agent."

"Which makes you the most suspicious of all," Alex said, grinning. Emma rolled her eyes, but her smirk gave her away. "Fine. I'll tell you about the time I accidentally joined a goat cult." Everyone blinked. "A *what?*" Jordan asked.

"A goat cult," she repeated, crossing her legs like she was about to give a TED Talk. "So, I signed up for what I *thought* was a weekend yoga retreat in the countryside. The ad said, 'Reconnect with nature. Embrace your inner peace. Special guests included.' I figured it was just some hippie nonsense with maybe a guest instructor and overpriced herbal tea."

"Sounds relaxing so far," Ivy said.

"Oh, it started that way," Emma nodded. "I got there, and the place looked legit, rolling hills, cozy cabins, lots of fresh air. But then I saw the goats. Dozens of them. Wearing flower crowns."

"No," Andrew squinted, already laughing. "Yes. They were just... everywhere. On yoga mats. In the dining hall. One even tried to climb into my luggage. I thought maybe it was just an eccentric farm vibe. But then came the welcome ceremony." Alina leaned forward, clearly intrigued.

"They handed everyone a white robe," Emma continued, "and led us into this candlelit barn. Everyone started chanting. I was like, okay, group bonding, whatever. Then the leader walks in, barefoot, bearded, eyes sparkling with... goat energy, and says, 'We must now give thanks to our guide and guardian... Prince Fluff.'"

"Who's Prince Fluff?" Alex asked cautiously. Emma grinned. "A goat. A large, mildly aggressive goat who trotted in wearing a velvet cape and tiny golden boots. Everyone bowed. I just stood there, frozen, wondering if I'd accidentally joined an animal-themed cult." The group burst into uncontrollable laughter. "So what did you do?" Ivy asked, wiping a tear from her eye.

"I bowed," Emma said flatly. "I panicked. The goat was staring me down. I wasn't about to get headbutted by royalty. I bowed and pretended like I knew what I was doing. I made it through the weekend, survived a sacred cheese ceremony, and escaped during the 'Moon-rise Bleating Blessing' ritual."

Jordan was laughing so hard he wheezed. "You survived a goat cult!" Emma held up a hand like a badge. "I did. And I still get emails from them. Apparently, I'm a 'lifetime initiate of the wool-bound path.'"

"And the moral of your story?" Andrew asked, nearly in tears. Emma took a deep breath. "Always read the *entire* retreat description. Especially the fine print under 'special guests.'"

As the laughter over the goat cult slowly subsided, all eyes turned to Liam. He stretched, cracked his knuckles, and said, "Alright, alright. I guess it's my turn. But let me warn you, mine doesn't involve volcanoes, goat royalty, or criminal tofu. Mine involves… pants."

Jordan groaned. "Oh no. Is this the daycare incident?" Liam pointed at him. "You keep your mouth shut. Let me tell it." He turned to the group with the flair of a man both proud and eternally scarred.

"So, I was off-duty, helping my sister with her twins. She begs me to pick them up from daycare because she's stuck in traffic. I say sure. Easy. No big deal. I show up, two sleepy kids, one sticky from grape jelly, the other wearing a tiara and a serious attitude. I carry one in each arm, juggling their bags like a pro."

"So far, so good," Emma said. "I get to the car, put them in their car seats, and that's when I feel it, the unmistakable *rrriiippp*." Everyone winced.

"Yeah. Back of my pants. Gone. Like the Grand Canyon. I'm in the daycare parking lot, crouched down, and now I'm moonlighting, literally. And guess what? It was Pajama Day at the daycare. All the staff are outside, all the parents are outside, and suddenly, I'm the entertainment."

Alina was laughing now, hiding her face behind her hand. "I try to back into the car like it's no big deal, but one of the toddlers yells, 'I see your underwear!' And the worst part? I was wearing my lucky boxers. The ones that say 'Liam the Lion' with an actual cartoon lion roaring across the back."

The group erupted with laughter. "Lesson learned," Liam concluded. "Never ignore the small tear in your pants. It's a warning. Respect it." As the laughter faded again, Emma leaned toward Ivy, eyes gleaming. "Alright, Ivy. You're the last one. Give us something good."

"Yeah," Alex said, pointing at her. "You've been quiet too long." Ivy looked around the circle, then smiled softly, her eyes distant with nostalgia. "Okay… I'll tell you a story. One with my dad." The group leaned in.

"I was about eight," she began. "We were on this camping trip, just me and my father. He wanted to teach me 'survival skills.' I was excited… until I realized his idea of 'roughing it' included a fully packed RV, marshmallows the size of softballs, and a Bluetooth speaker that played Frank Sinatra in the middle of the woods." Andrew chuckled. "Classic dad move."

"So, the first night, he tells me we're going to catch our own dinner, like true pioneers. We have fishing rods, bait, the whole setup. After two hours of not catching anything, I'm starving. I suggest maybe we just open the cooler, but no, he insists nature will provide."

"And did it?" Alina asked. Ivy grinned. "Sort of. I finally get a bite. I reel it in like a champ. My dad's cheering like I just won gold at the Olympics. And when I pull it out… it's a shoe." Laughter exploded around the circle. "An actual muddy, mossy, old hiking boot. Size 11. I looked at it, looked at my dad, and said, 'Should we grill it with garlic or lemon?'" Everyone laughed harder.

"But my dad didn't miss a beat. He claps his hands and goes, 'Perfect. Tonight we dine like ancient warriors, on Sole!' And he actually made a little fire ceremony around it. We placed the shoe on a rock like it was sacred. He even gave it a name. Sir Bootsworth." Jordan was howling. "Please tell me you still have the shoe!"

"No," Ivy said, laughing, "but we did take a picture of it, and he kept it in his wallet for years. Told everyone it was the only fish I ever caught." The group melted into laughter, but their smiles softened as they saw the shimmer in Ivy's eyes, joyful and touched with memory.

She looked at the fire, her voice quieter now. "He made everything magical, even the dumbest things. And somehow, every bad situation turned into the best memory." No one spoke for a moment. Then Liam raised his glass. "To, Sir Bootsworth."

Everyone echoed it with laughter, clinking glasses under the stars, bound by friendship, stories, and the warmth of shared wonder.

Emma raised her glass. "To unexpected friendships and wild journeys, whether they're to attics or the moon." Everyone laughed and toasted.

As the sun set and the first stars appeared, Ivy found herself standing quietly by the fence, looking up. Alina walked over and joined her. "You're thinking about him," Alina said softly.

Ivy nodded. "Always. Ethan says I'm getting close." Alina smiled gently. "You'll get there. And when you do, he'll be waiting." Liam walked over and slipped his arm around Ivy's shoulders. "Everything okay?" Ivy leaned into him and smiled. "Yeah. Just appreciating this moment."

The soft murmur of conversation and laughter continued behind them, a reminder that even as Ivy prepared to cross into extraordinary realms once again, life's simplest moments still held the deepest magic.

The next evening, after the warmth of the weekend had faded into a cool, starlit sky, Ivy sat alone in her apartment, the faint scent of barbecue smoke still lingering in her clothes. She closed her eyes and inhaled deeply, centering herself.

Within moments, her spirit slipped free. The room faded, replaced by the familiar silver-blue expanse of the spirit plane. Ethan stood waiting, his expression more serious than usual. Alina appeared moments later, materializing beside him with her calm, knowing presence. "You're ready," Ethan said quietly. "If you still want to go, it's time to begin the final preparations." Ivy nodded without hesitation. "I want to see my father."

Ethan gave her a rare, soft smile. "Then we have work to do." They walked together through the glowing landscape. Strange, crystalline structures rose around them like ancient monuments. The air hummed softly with energy.

"The place where your father rests," Ethan explained, "exists deeper within the spirit realm. It's safe, but very few ever cross that far and return. It's called the Luminous Sanctuary. To reach it, your spirit must be strong, steady, and completely untethered by fear."

Alina added softly, "This is not just about the strength of body, Ivy. It's about clarity of intention and the purity of your bond with your father."

Ethan led Ivy through a series of increasingly difficult exercises: walking across flowing rivers of energy without losing her form, resisting disorienting storms of fragmented memories that tried to pull her back toward the living world, and learning to hear the distant pulse that marked the pathway to the Sanctuary.

At times, Ethan would step back and watch her progress with hidden admiration. When Ivy stumbled or faltered, Alina's soothing voice would guide her back to focus. "You're remarkable," Ethan said one evening as Ivy balanced in the center of a swirling vortex of energy. "Most would have given up by now." Ivy smiled faintly, determination burning in her eyes. "I told you. I'm not leaving without seeing him."

As they rested after another intense session, Alina drifted off briefly. Ethan turned to Ivy, glancing playfully toward the faint tether of Emma's energy far off in the living world.

"You know," Ethan said with a half-smirk, "if I ever return to a full physical life, you *are* going to introduce me to Emma properly. There's just something about her. A sharp mind and no fear of the unknown? That's rare."

Ivy laughed, genuinely this time, shaking her head. "I'll think about it. You're both impossible."

Ethan gave her a wink. "I'm persistent." The mood grew quiet as Ivy looked to the distance, where faint shimmering lights marked the edge of the deeper realm.

"How much longer?" she asked softly.

Ethan's tone softened. "Soon. One more crossing. When you're ready, I will guide you to him." Ivy nodded, her heart full of anticipation and quiet gratitude for the unlikely friendships she had found along the way.

The night arrived quietly. Ivy stood at her apartment window, the moon casting a silver glow across the city. The world below continued in its usual rhythm, unaware of the extraordinary journey about to unfold. Emma sat cross-legged nearby, watching Ivy light a single white candle. "Are you sure about this?" Emma whispered.

Ivy smiled calmly. "I've never been more sure of anything."

Emma reached over and squeezed Ivy's hand. "Be safe. And tell him… tell your dad I said thank you. For giving me my friend back."

Ivy's heart softened at the words. She nodded, closed her eyes, and began the familiar breath-work that bridged her to the spirit plane.

The world dissolved into flowing silver and deep indigo light. Ethan and Alina were already waiting, their forms vibrant and steady against the shifting energies around them. Ethan's expression held a mix of pride and concern.

"This is it," Ethan said gently. "Beyond this point, I cannot go with you. Only you and your father share the bond needed to cross into the Sanctuary."

Alina touched Ivy's arm with serene strength. "We will wait here and guard your return."

Ivy stood tall, feeling the weight of her training and the pull of her heart. "I understand." Ethan stepped closer, his tone softening. "You've already done the impossible, Ivy. No matter what happens, remember, you're loved in both worlds."

With a final nod, Ivy turned toward the shimmering rift that had appeared ahead of her. It pulsed like a heartbeat, calling to her across the veil. She stepped forward. The moment her spirit crossed the threshold, the world transformed.

The Luminous Sanctuary unfolded before her like something out of legend: rolling fields of soft golden mist, crystalline trees that rang like distant chimes when the breeze touched them, and towering spires of radiant light rising into infinity. It was both overwhelming and deeply peaceful.

In the center of the field stood a familiar figure, strong and tall, yet filled with gentle warmth. Cyrus. "Dad…" Ivy whispered.

Cyrus turned and smiled, tears forming in his radiant eyes. "Ivy?"

She ran to him, their spirit forms embracing tightly in a reunion that defied time and mortality. Cyrus stroked her hair just as he had when she was a child. "I've missed you so much," Ivy sobbed.

"And I've watched over you every day," Cyrus said tenderly. "You are stronger than I ever dreamed, my beautiful girl."

They sat together beneath the glowing spires, talking for what felt like hours. Ivy told him everything: her recovery, the mysterious messages, Ethan and Alina's help, Emma's friendship, and her own journey into the spirit realm.

Cyrus listened with wonder and pride. "You've found your family, Ivy. Not just the one you were born into, but the ones you've chosen."

As the golden mist began to pulse softly, a sign that the crossing window was closing, Cyrus held her tightly once more. "Can't I stay?" Ivy asked, her voice breaking.

"Not yet," Cyrus whispered. "You belong to the living world. You still have so much more to do. But we will meet again, when it's time."

Ivy looked at him, eyes shimmering with longing. "Dad… why was it so hard to see you here?"

Cyrus touched her cheek gently. "This wall was created by your own heart, the sorrow you held, the tears you shed, the anger you carried against the world. When peace finds you, when your soul is calm, I'll be able to cross more easily. And then… I'll be right here."

With tears in her eyes and love swelling in her heart, Ivy stepped back. The Sanctuary slowly faded, and the light pulled her gently home. Back in her apartment, Ivy awoke with a soft gasp. Emma was at her side instantly. "Ivy? Are you okay?"

Ivy smiled through tears of joy. "I saw him, Emma. I held him. I told him everything." Emma threw her arms around her. "I'm so happy for you." As Ivy breathed in the scent of the candle and the soft nighttime breeze, she knew her journey was far from over, but she had found peace in a way she never thought possible.

The next morning, Ivy and Emma sat together on the small balcony of Ivy's apartment, sipping tea as the city slowly came alive under the soft pink hue of sunrise. Emma studied her friend with a half-smile. "You look different," she said. "Peaceful. Lighter." Ivy nodded, eyes distant but calm. "I feel like I've been carrying a weight for so long… and last night I finally put it down."

Emma smiled warmly and reached over to squeeze Ivy's hand. "I'm glad, Ivy. Truly." Ivy hesitated for a moment, then glanced sideways at her friend with a mischievous twinkle. "There's something else I should tell you."

Emma raised an eyebrow. "Oh no. That tone usually means trouble."

Ivy laughed. "Not trouble. More like… potential." She took a breath. "Ethan likes you."

Emma blinked. "Wait. *Ethan?* As in your mysterious spirit guide, walk-between-worlds, Ethan?"

"The very same." Ivy nodded. "And not just in a vague spirit-being way. I mean, really. He watches over me, yes, but he notices you. Your humor, your loyalty… even the way you sneak snacks before yoga class." Emma flushed, half-embarrassed, half-intrigued. "That's ridiculous. He's a… I don't even know what he is!"

Ivy laughed. "He's alive, Emma. His body's out there somewhere. He can travel in spirit, but he's very real. I told you, he even joked about asking you out if he ever comes back fully."

Emma stared at her, stunned, then burst into laughter. "You're serious?"

Ivy nodded. "Completely. And I think… if you ever want to understand any of this deeper, if you're even a little curious, you should push yourself a bit more in yoga. Alina and I both think you've got a natural sensitivity. You're already halfway there without realizing it."

Emma tilted her head thoughtfully, still grinning. "So let me get this straight. You want me to level up my yoga skills so I can flirt with an inter-dimensional spirit traveler?"

Ivy shrugged playfully. "Stranger things have happened. Besides, you might find answers of your own along the way."

Emma shook her head, still smiling. "You're unbelievable."

Ivy winked. "And yet here you are." As the two friends laughed under the early morning sky, across the unseen veil, Ethan watched them, an amused smile on his face. Alina drifted quietly beside him, sharing a knowing glance.

"She's going to be trouble, isn't she?" Ethan murmured.

Alina smiled softly. "The best kind."

After work, Ivy and Emma were once again on their way to the yoga centre, it had started to feel like a second home. Alina had begun the second phase of their training, emphasizing the importance of focus in mastering yoga. Mid-lesson, while Alina spoke, Ivy was already ahead, flowing through the sequence with quiet precision. She turned and spotted Ethan watching her. He smiled, clearly impressed.

"You're mastering it," he said, surprised. "Every time, you're faster than the last. I'm impressed."

Ivy smiled back. "When you have a reason for something, you master it."

Ethan nodded. "That's true."

Everything shimmered around Ivy, the air, the thoughts, the space between moments. In this state, her body remained seated in a flawless meditative pose, motionless and serene, while her soul had slipped free, fluid, weightless, and unseen. Time no longer concerned her; even if she wandered for days through that otherworldly realm, only minutes would pass on Earth.

She moved effortlessly among them, a silent observer. No one could hear her. Not even Emma, who sat with closed eyes, her brow furrowed in concentration. Ivy's spirit leaned in close, sensing her friend's flicker of self-doubt. *Maybe I'll never be able to do it the way Ivy does.* The thought echoed gently, tinged with sadness.

Ivy couldn't respond, not with words. But she let her energy speak, letting a wave of warmth brush past Emma like a breeze of encouragement, soft and invisible. Emma stirred slightly and took a deeper breath, as if something had just lifted her heart.

Ethan, across the room, paused mid-step. He turned slowly, his eyes narrowing. He couldn't see her, but something in him reacted, like a quiet bell ringing in his chest.

Alina raised her voice again. "Return your awareness to the room. Breathe in. Breathe out. Let yourself come back." Gradually, Ivy's spirit drifted back into her body. With a single breath, her eyes fluttered open. She felt calm, centered, and glowing.

Emma turned to her with a quiet smile. "I don't know why, but... something just felt different. Better." Ivy smiled gently, her eyes distant, glowing with an inner stillness.

Emma watched her for a moment, then tilted her head. Ivy wasn't blinking. She wasn't moving. Her body was there, perfectly composed, but her presence. It felt... absent. A chill of awe passed through Emma.

She's not here, Emma thought. *Her soul must be on an adventure now.*

She looked around, no one else seeming to notice. Alina continued her lesson, and the others breathed and stretched in silence. But Emma knew. Quietly, with care, she settled back into her seat and closed her eyes. *One day,* she whispered in her mind, *I'll find a way to follow.*

When souls are on the other side, time no longer matters. Minutes, hours, even years blur into one still, weightless silence.

Ivy floated just beyond her body, her form shimmering with a soft, silver light. Beside her, Ethan's spirit hovered, steady and calm. Everything below, the yoga centre, the students, the world seemed like a distant hum.

"Do you think we should wait for Alina?" Ethan asked, his voice like a thought carried on the wind. Ivy turned her gaze. Alina was still seated, eyes closed, speaking in a low, rhythmic tone to guide the others. Her spirit remained anchored, untouched. Ivy looked around Emma, the others, they were still grounded, their souls tethered tightly inside their bodies.

She was the only one who had crossed over. The realization warmed her from within. A quiet pride rose in her, earned, not given. "No," Ivy said, her voice glowing with resolve. "Let's go. We'll come back for Alina later." Ethan nodded. "Let's go." And with that, their forms slipped forward, leaving the room behind like a dream fading into morning.

Ethan followed Ivy closely, the two of them soaring like weightless children, weaving and tumbling through layers of soft, golden clouds. Ivy laughed with pure delight, the sound echoing in a way only souls could hear. She twisted midair, looping around Ethan with a grin as wide as the sky itself.

"Where do you want to go today?" Ethan asked, drifting closer, his voice playful.

Ivy's eyes sparkled as she shot upward, slicing through a cloud like light through silk. She didn't answer right away, caught in the thrill of it. Then, breathless with joy, she turned and asked, "Are we able to go inside the sun?"

Ethan burst into laughter. "That was the first thing I did! It's wild, burns without pain, blinds without darkness. It's... intense."

Ivy looked around, her gaze sweeping the glowing horizon. "How about *around* the sun? Let's go around it!"

Without waiting for an answer, she dove forward, and Ethan followed. Together they spiraled toward the burning giant, the solar flares dancing around them like ribbons of fire. They passed through it, fluid and untouched, and emerged on the other side in a burst of glowing silence.

Ivy slowed, blinking. Everything looked... the same. "We made a mistake," she said, confused. "We're still on the same side." Ethan floated beside her, smiling knowingly.

"No, we're not." Ivy frowned, glancing around.

"No one has ever seen the *other* side of the sun," he continued. "I mean, we just did. But not many understand what that means. Earth is always moving around it, right? But exactly on the other side... there's another planet. Just like Earth. Same size, same orbit. Same speed, like a twin sister. Only the map is a little different."

Ivy's breath caught. "What?"

"It's a blue planet too," Ethan said, voice low and serious now. "I call it Earth's sister. But you have to keep it to yourself."

"But… why?" Ivy asked, her voice laced with confusion and a flicker of fear.

Ethan looked at her, his expression darkening just a little. "Because they already know. And what do you think all these UFOs are coming from? They can't all be from distant galaxies." He drifted closer, his voice dropping lower.

"They're from *here*, Ivy. From the other side of the sun. From that sister planet. Their technology isn't just advanced, it's thousands of years ahead of us. They live in harmony, in peace. No wars. No division. They've never turned against each other. That's why their world feels like heaven."

Ivy's eyes widened, stunned by the truth unraveling before her. Ethan's tone sharpened. "But if you tell anyone… if you even whisper a word of it on Earth…" He paused. "You'll be in big trouble. The kind of trouble that wakes up the Watchers."

Ivy drifted forward, her soul drawn toward the blue planet shimmering just beyond the sun's reach. It looked so familiar, clouds, oceans, continents shaped like memories, but something in the air felt different. Calmer. Older. Wiser.

She didn't know what she might face, but she moved gently, silently descending through the atmosphere. As she passed over cities and villages, she saw people. People who looked just like those on Earth, only there was something distinct in their expressions. A quiet pride. Not arrogance, but dignity. Peace without indifference. Purpose without pressure.

She floated through their communities, observing without being seen. Everywhere she looked, life thrived, not in excess, but in balance. The homes blended with nature, the skies were clear, the waters glowed with purity. Laughter echoed, not from chaos, but from contentment.

There was no crowding. No frantic movement. The planet wasn't overpopulated because its people didn't chase numbers. They protected their space, cherished their air, and lived with intention.

And the cleanliness, beyond anything Ivy had imagined. There was hardly any waste. No rotting piles of forgotten things. No toxins seeping into soil. Everything was repurposed, reused, or respectfully returned to the earth. Even the tires of their vehicles were unlike anything on Earth, crafted from a strange iron alloy and filled with intricate networks of springs hidden within. The result was a ride so fluid, it seemed to glide rather than roll.

"God," Ivy muttered, watching in awe, "their cars move ninety percent smoother than ours. How is that even possible?"

This, Ivy thought, *is what they mean when they say no one goes to bed hungry.*

Not merely fed with food, but with peace. With belonging. With a life that finally made sense. Tears shimmered in her eyes, but they refused to fall, not here. Here, even emotions felt weightless, drifting like whispers through cities, winding roads, golden fields, silent mountains, and mirror-like lakes. It was the most beautiful world Ivy could ever have imagined.

They arrived at an island hidden in the heart of the ocean, so breathtakingly beautiful that, upon landing, they stood in stunned silence. The landscape was otherworldly, a vision too perfect to belong to Earth. Ivy finally turned to Ethan and asked, "Have you been here before?"

Ethan smiled and gave a quiet nod. "I told you I had. When I need peace, I come here to watch them. If people on Earth felt even a fraction of the responsibility these beings do, our world could be just as harmonious. But sadly, most only think of themselves, even if their actions leave someone else in ruins."

Without meeting his gaze, she murmured, "We should tell people about this place. They have the right to know."

Ethan rose slowly, his eyes steady on hers. "We can't," he said. "We must leave it untouched. The scientists here… they're beyond anything we've ever seen. Clearly, they don't want us to know about this place, or about them. And our government… they already suspect. They've known for a long time that something's out here. If we disturb the sister planet, they won't take it lightly. And the terrifying part? They've restarted life on Earth, wiped it clean, more times than we can count. They have that power.

Ivy hugged her knees, her voice soft and distant. "Do you think Earth will ever find out about this second Earth?" Ethan didn't answer. Silence stretched between them.

She continued, "How could they? When both Earths are the same distance from the Sun, perfectly aligned, hiding in plain sight. But look at this place… "If our world had never known war or man-made religions, perhaps we too could have nurtured such beauty, unspoiled, harmonious, and whole."

Ethan smiled faintly. "Absolutely. War and religion have always stood in the way of true human advancement, in both technology and quality of life. Just look at the world: whenever a dictator or a nation feels threatened, they ignite a war to distract the masses, to steer their minds away from progress and keep them focused on fear." She glanced at him, curious.

He went on, "Religion isn't from God. It's a system created by people to control others, to fuel the power of a few. A way to enslave minds, willingly. God doesn't need a religion to prove existence. God simply is, the creator of all. You don't need to search. You just need to see."

Ivy smiled gently. "But don't you need a guide to get closer to God?" Ethan kept his eyes on the horizon. "That idea," he said quietly, "was planted by those who rule, by the ones who built religions to control, not to enlighten."

He turned toward her. "Tell me, why would a perfect God need to send so many prophets, each with different messages, different laws, even ones that contradict each other? Isn't that strange? Just look at the religions of the world. In Roman Catholicism, priests are forbidden to marry. In Islam, men are allowed up to five wives, unlimited temporary marriages, and even the taking of captives as concubines after war. Each system has its own rituals, its own rules, its own version of what God supposedly desires. And yet, every one of them claims to be the only truth, that everyone else must convert or be condemned to hell. If that's the case, then according to each of them, we're all going to hell."

He paused, "What kind of God needs confusion to deliver the truth? Why are religious books written in ways so complex and contradictory that we need someone else to interpret them for us? Doesn't God understand human beings? Wouldn't a true creator know that 95% of people can't fully grasp the Bible, the Torah, or the Quran?"

He let the words sink in, then continued, "Maybe that's exactly why they wrote them that way, conflicting, obscure, and difficult to understand. It's all part of the business. Their business."

He drew a deep breath, then added, "Did you know some churches demand forty percent of your income? Even if you're struggling or filled with doubt, none of that matters as long as you pay. And if this is truly for God, why charge anything at all? Shouldn't it be done freely, out of love or faith, maybe in their spare time? But no… across all religions, it's the same. You have to pay. They get rich, live in luxury, and often don't even pay taxes."

Then he added, his voice steady, "Science doesn't work that way. If you eat rat poison, you die, that's a fact. No one can say it's safe just because another scientist has a different opinion. Science has rules. Math has rules. Two times two is four, always. Not five. Not thirteen."

He looked back at the sea. "So what kind of God sends thousands of messengers with thousands of conflicting commands, each claiming divine authority, often with the right to kill those who don't follow? What kind of God is that? A confused one? Or maybe just one created by men, powerful enough to control, but too flawed to make sense."

Ivy looked at him, startled. "You mean… there's no God?"

Ethan finally turned to face her, his gaze calm but firm. "What part of anything I said sounded like I don't believe in God?"

He moved closer and sat beside her, his voice softer now. "Finding God isn't complicated. People made it complicated. God's truth is simple, so simple that even a child can understand it: Don't lie. Don't hurt others. Don't judge. Help one another. And love, always love."

He paused, letting the silence between them speak. "That's all God ever wanted. The rest? That was man's doing."

Ivy looked sad then she stood up, her eyes shining with curiosity. "Let's go see the other cities. They must be even more beautiful."

Ethan smiled, rising beside her. "Let's go. I'm sure you'll be amazed."

They glided toward the next city. Every home they passed had its own generous space, surrounded by vibrant gardens and landscapes blooming with meticulously arranged flowers. The design of the land itself seemed like a living painting.

They approached a modest home where an elderly couple resided. The air was calm and serene, wrapped in a gentle stillness. "They don't have maids," Ethan said softly, "but they don't need them. Everything is taken care of. The system provides their food, keeps the house clean, and even arranges daily movement and walks for them, whatever they need, it's already done."

Ivy watched closely as the couple moved their hands gracefully through the air. Small, sleek devices on their wrists responded to their gestures, lifting a bowl of food from one table and guiding it gently to another. She was mesmerized. Then, just as the meal was set before them, the couple joined hands and bowed their heads, whispering a prayer of gratitude.

Ivy turned to Ethan, her eyes wide with surprise. "They pray… for their food? Even when everything is already provided?"

Ethan nodded, a gentle smile touching his lips. "Of course they do. They believe in the true God, not a business God, not the kind people use to show off in public while hiding cruelty in private. They don't parade their faith through the streets. They live it quietly, with peace, gratitude, and love."

Ivy smiled, eyes narrowing playfully. "You know a lot about these people. You must've been here often."

Ethan gave her a contented smile, a warm glint in his eyes. "Yup. I love the way they live here. It's peaceful, deeply peaceful, and, somehow, everything just feels… right. They don't even know what a lie is, because they always choose what's right, not what's more profitable. It's like a dreamland."

Ethan looked at her, his expression turning serious. "We should go back. You shouldn't stay out of your body for too long."

Ivy tilted her head, curious. "Why not? What happens if I do?"

He walked to the window, gazing out for a moment before replying, "The longer you stay out, the harder it becomes to return. Your connection weakens. If you don't go back in time… you might not be able to return at all."

Ivy smiled faintly, a trace of peace on her lips. "I don't mind. I don't want to go back to that life anyway."

Ethan's smile mirrored hers, but his eyes held something heavier. He gently took her hand and, as he began to pull her with him, said softly, "Honey, if you stay… it counts as suicide. And if that happens, you won't see your father again. You won't see God, you'll meet the god of hell."

Ivy's face changed, her smile fading into alarm. "You're joking, right?"

"I wish I were," Ethan said quietly. "But it's the truth. So please… be careful."

Ivy looked around, her heart racing. She turned to Ethan one last time, and in the blink of an eye, she was back in her body. She opened her eyes to the blinding lights and the wail of sirens. The ceiling above her was moving, no, she was moving. She was in an ambulance, speeding through the night. Emma was beside her, sobbing uncontrollably.

Ivy reached out and grabbed Emma's hand. "What's happening?" she whispered, her voice barely audible.

Emma gasped, then threw her arms around her in a half-hug, half-collapse of relief. "She's awake! She's awake!" she cried, turning to the paramedic.

The paramedic immediately leaned over, taking Ivy's wrist to check her pulse. "Ivy, can you hear me?" he asked urgently. "How do you feel? Don't close your eyes, stay with me. Talk to me, Ivy. Stay awake."

"I'm okay, I'm okay," Ivy kept repeating, her voice still weak but steady.

She turned to Emma, her brows furrowed. "What happened, Emma? Why am I here?"

Emma wiped her tears, trying to calm her breathing. "You collapsed, Ivy. You just fell. No matter what we did, shaking you, calling your name, you wouldn't wake up. We tried everything."

Ivy gave a faint smile, as if remembering something far away. "Where's Alina?"

Emma let out a breath, her voice steadier now. "Alina got an emergency call. I think her mom's sick, she had to leave right away."

Ivy smiled faintly at Emma. "That's why I'm here. If Alina had been there, she would've known exactly what to do." She then turned to the paramedic. "I'm okay. I promise. Would you please take us back?" The paramedic shook his head gently. "You still need to be checked out at the hospital, just to be sure everything's alright."

"I understand," Ivy said softly, "but please… can you return us? I'm really okay. I promise."

The paramedic hesitated, studying her face, then picked up his radio and made a quick call. After a brief exchange, he looked back at her. "I can't take you back. We've been dispatched to pick up another patient. But I can drop you off at the hospital. From there, you're free to get checked out or return to wherever you were."

Ivy sat upright on the stretcher, turning to Emma with a soft smile. Today had been a day full of surprises, some strange, some beautiful, all unforgettable. As they stepped out of the ambulance in front of the hospital, Ivy's eyes caught a familiar figure rushing toward the emergency doors.

"Liam! Liam!" she called out, her voice cutting through the noise.

He turned abruptly, eyes wide with disbelief. The moment he saw her, he hurried toward her, and Ivy ran straight into his arms, wrapping him in a hug so tight it felt like she never wanted to let go.

"What happened? Are you okay?" Liam asked, his voice thick with concern.

Ivy pulled back slightly, still holding onto him. "What are you doing here?"

Liam glanced at Emma, then looked back at Ivy. "Emma called me. She told me you collapsed and weren't waking up. She told me which hospital they were bringing you to, I came right away."

His shoulders eased as he searched her eyes. "Are you alright now?"

"I'm okay," Ivy whispered. "Let's go home." She looked exhausted.

Liam nodded and drove them both to Ivy's place. After making sure she was settled, he quietly left. Inside, Ivy and Emma stepped into the calm, familiar warmth of the house. Ivy collapsed onto the couch and began recounting everything that had happened, everything except the truth about the second Earth. Ethan had made her promise to keep that part hidden.

Emma listened intently, her eyes wide with wonder. When Ivy finished, Emma couldn't contain her excitement. "This is incredible! I'm going to try even harder. I want to go with you next time. I'm so excited!"

But the next day was a different story. Ivy had spent most of the morning drifting through dreams, her mind caught somewhere between reality and everything else she had seen. Vincent, her supervisor, was clearly not pleased. He called her into his office, his expression heavy with concern. As she stepped inside, he placed a file on the desk in front of her and met her eyes.

"Ivy, you seem really distracted lately," he said, disappointment in his voice. "Is everything alright? Do you need help? This file was due yesterday. It's still sitting on your desk."

Ivy's heart sank. She had never been late on a project before. Her work was always precise, always timely. But lately, her world had become... different. Too surreal to explain. She'd lost her focus, floating through her days like she wasn't quite there.

"I'm sorry, Vincent," she said quietly. "I'll finish it today. It's a promise."

Vincent's expression softened. He knew how dependable she was. He nodded and slid the file back toward her with a faint smile. "Tomorrow morning, when I come into my office, I want to see it done on my desk."

Ivy gave a small smile in return. "Of course. Thank you." She stayed after hours, determined to keep her promise.

The office was quiet, the hum of distant traffic barely audible through the windows as Ivy focused on her work, her fingers gliding across the keyboard, when Emma stepped into the office, her voice hopeful. "Are you ready?"

Ivy looked up with an apologetic smile. "I'm sorry, Emma. Not tonight. I have to finish this file, I promised Vincent it would be ready by morning."

Emma's expression fell. "But without you, it's hard now. With you, I have more courage to do it… but I don't know about tonight." Without another word, she turned and walked away, leaving Ivy alone in the quiet room.

Ivy didn't hesitate. She took a breath, pushed aside the guilt tugging at her, and focused. There was no time to waste. She organized her thoughts, checked every detail, and made sure everything was in perfect order.

Her attention was locked on the task, pouring herself into the file for Vincent. Every piece of data, every line of research, had to be exact. She was entering notes onto a separate sheet, her focus razor-sharp, until her cellphone rang. The sudden sound broke her concentration. She glanced at the screen. An unknown number. Her heart skipped. Could it be her father again?

The phone kept ringing. She answered it, but there was nothing, no sound, no voice, just silence. Ivy lowered the phone, staring at it with unease. Then she stood in the middle of the dim office, the glow of the computer screen behind her, and said firmly into the stillness, "Whoever you are, I'm very busy tonight. Please let me be, and leave me alone."

There was no sound on the other end, just a dead silence that faded into the stillness of the room. Shaking it off, Ivy turned back to her work and continued without distraction until the final detail was complete.

She sat back and looked at the file with quiet pride, as if it were a piece of her soul laid bare on paper. She had held on, kept her promise, and poured herself into it. For a moment, she simply stared at it, as if trying to etch it into her memory forever. Gently, she placed the file on Vincent's desk, then gathered her things and prepared to leave. Just as she reached for her coat, her cellphone rang, this time violently, as if trying to shake the quiet night apart.

She grabbed it and quickly answered, "Hello?" There was a pause, then Liam's voice came through, steady and familiar. "Hi, Ivy. Do you know what time it is? It's passed 10.30. Where are you?"

Her face lit up with a tired but happy smile. "I'm at the office. I promised Vincent I'd finish the project I was supposed to complete yesterday, so I stayed late. Where are you?"

His voice softened. "I'm in front of your house and see your car parked there. Wait for me, I'll be at the office in ten minutes to pick you up."

A wave of relief washed over her. "Okay," she said with a smile. "I'll see you soon."

In the morning, Ivy was at the printer, gathering pages into a neat stack, when Emma walked in. "How do you feel, Ivy?" she asked.

Ivy looked up, her face glowing with energy. "I couldn't be better," she said, her voice light and confident.

She stepped closer, leaned in, and whispered in Emma's ear with a mischievous glint in her eye, "I can't wait to go on another unforgettable journey tonight. These experiences… they're completely out of this world. You can't even imagine them, unless you've been there yourself."

Emma smiled bitterly, her eyes searching Ivy's face. "I'm trying," she said softly. "And I hope I can join you guys someday."

Ivy gave her a playful wink. "Don't worry. Sooner or later, you'll be there, I'm sure of it."

By 3:30, Ivy could hardly sit still. Her eyes kept darting to the clock, counting down each second like it held a secret. Finally, Emma opened her office door and leaned in with a grin. "Are you ready?"

Ivy sprang to her feet, grabbing her things with the excitement of someone chasing a dream. "I was ready yesterday." Both of them burst into laughter, the kind that bubbles up from shared hope and anticipation.

They reached Alina's yoga studio, where soft music floated through the air and the scent of lavender lingered. Alina was chatting with a few members near the entrance, but as soon as she spotted Ivy and Emma, her expression lit up with concern and excitement. She hurried over. "I heard you were in the hospital yesterday! What happened?"

Ivy smiled calmly, then glanced at Emma with a playful spark in her eye before turning to Alina. "If you had been here, that never would've happened," she said teasingly, nodding toward Emma. "She completely panicked when I collapsed, didn't know what to do. Froze like a statue. Poor thing was scared out of her mind."

Alina took both their hands and gently tugged them forward. "Come on in, we'll start in a minute." Emma and Ivy exchanged a quick glance, then hurried to the lockers to drop off their belongings. In moments, they returned, unrolled their mats, and settled into the poised, grounded position yoga demanded.

Alina moved to the front of the room, her presence calm and centered. She looked at Ivy with a knowing smile. "By the way, Ethan told me about the incredible trip you had yesterday. We'll talk about it later." Ivy's eyes sparkled as she nodded, her smile warm and brimming with anticipation, while Emma watched her with wide-eyed excitement.

Alina stepped to the front of the class, her voice calm and inviting. "Listen, everyone, we have three new members today. I'm glad to introduce them to you, and I'd like them to share a little about themselves…" Her words began to blur, drifting like an echo in Ivy's ears. The room seemed to fade as a familiar voice pierced through the soft hum of background sound.

CHAPTER FOUR – Trust Unraveled

"You're getting faster. How do you do that this fast?" Ivy turned sharply, her eyes wide. Ethan stood behind her, relaxed and amused. "What?" she whispered. "When did you come in?"

Ethan smiled, tilting his head slightly. "I'm not here physically," he said, his voice low and steady. "And neither are you. You're not in your body right now." Ivy glanced down and gasped softly. There she was, still sitting cross-legged beside Emma, perfectly still, her eyes closed in serene focus. Emma remained unaware, listening attentively to the new members as they spoke.

Alina, however, wasn't fooled. Her gaze rested not on Ivy's body, but just above it, into the invisible air where Ivy now stood beside Ethan. A knowing smile curved Alina's lips, and she gave a slow, deliberate nod, as if to say, *I see you. I know where you are.* It was clear now, Alina understood. They had entered the spirit world once again.

Ivy smiled, her arms outstretched as she soared through the endless skies of the spirit world. The wind of nothingness rushed past her, and she laughed with pure delight, shouting, "*Weeeee!*" Her voice echoed through the invisible planes. For nearly an hour, she and Ethan darted across realms, weightless and unbound. Here, tiredness didn't exist. The spirit world knew no limits.

Finally, Ethan slowed beside her, his voice soft and gentle. "Do you want to go back to the second Earth?" But Ivy shook her head slowly, silently refusing the idea.

Surprised, Ethan hovered in place. "Why not? I thought you liked that place." Ivy's expression shifted. Her eyes clouded with something deeper, an ache. "I *do* like that place," she said, her voice softer now. "But… I'm jealous of them."

She looked out over the shimmering ether and continued, "They're exactly like us, but look at what they've built. No war. No made-up religions dividing people. Everyone grows up with support, from the moment they're born until the end. No one sleeps on the street. No one starves. No dictators. No borders. They focus on science, on truth, on unity."

She turned to Ethan, her brow furrowed with curiosity. "How do you know there wasn't any war or religion there?" she asked, a hint of disbelief in her voice.

Ethan gazed toward the distant horizon, his expression calm but reflective. Then he looked back at her and said, "Because I studied in one of their schools for a year, specifically their planetary history. They've never had war, not even once. And religion as we know it? It never existed there."

Ivy looked at him in surprise. "You went to school there?"

Ethan smiled and said, "Not physically. But I was in their classroom, watching as the students learned about their history." He paused for a moment, then added, "You know, their belief in God runs deep. Every one of them. They pray each morning or at night, even pause before meals to thank God, and they do it with sincerity. Not out of fear of hell or hope for heaven, but simply because they love God. It's woven into their lives, not from fear, but from love."

Ivy listened in silence as Ethan continued. "They've been watching our planet for a long time, thousands of years, I'd say. They saw the chaos, wars, executions, endless divisions caused by religion, racism, sexism, the greed of the wealthy, the suffering of the poor, the obsession with money. They teach their children from the beginning how inhumane our way of life is. And in contrast, they teach them how to protect their planet, how to care for each other."

He looked into Ivy's eyes. "That's how I know."

Ivy's face fell, her joy dimmed by the weight of sorrow. "I hope our Earth never finds them," she whispered. "I don't want their peace to collapse. Do you think if our government ever found out about them... they'd try to attack?"

Ethan suddenly burst into laughter, not mockingly, but with a kind of incredulous amusement. "Attack them?" he said between chuckles. "We *can't.*"

He shook his head, eyes gleaming with the truth. "They're not stupid, Ivy. They could erase our planet by pressing a button, and we wouldn't even know where it came from. Their science is more than ten thousand years ahead of ours. While countries on our Earth were still fighting over land, slaves, and imaginary borders, they were already mapping energy fields and mastering time-space technology."

He looked at her with calm certainty. "They watched us destroy one another, and while we did, they chose a different path. To them, our planet is savage and primitive."

Ivy was gazing into the distance when, suddenly, her heart leapt, her father stood before her. She rushed to him and threw her arms around him. "Dad, you can come here now! I'm so happy!"

Cyrus smiled warmly, his voice calm and steady. "Yes, me too."

Ethan, watching them with a hint of curiosity, tilted his head and asked, "Cyrus… that name sounds familiar. Isn't that like the character in *Harry Potter*? Sirius something?"

Ivy burst out laughing, the sound echoing with joy. "That's *Sirius Black*, Ethan, Harry Potter's godfather." She then looked at her father with pride. "But my dad's name is *Cyrus*. He was named after Cyrus the Great, the king of ancient Persia, the only ruler in human history who built an empire on real human laws."

She turned to Ethan, her voice deepening with reverence. "Two thousand five hundred years ago, he ruled with principles that even today we struggle to uphold. Freedom of speech, freedom of religion, even freedom of sexuality, he established them all. When he conquered nations, he didn't enslave them; he freed them. He released people from their cruel rulers, forbade his soldiers from harming civilians, and commanded them to rebuild the sacred places of those they had liberated.

The very concept of human rights, what we now consider modern and civilized, is rooted in his code. And yet, not even in today's so-called advanced world have we reached what he achieved back then. He was the only man in power who truly cared for the people."

Ethan stood silent for a moment, clearly moved. "I had no idea about this king," he said quietly. "He must've been extraordinary. I'm going to study about him."

Cyrus turned to his daughter, pride shining in his eyes. "You've learned it well," he said warmly. "I'm so proud of you."

Ivy beamed at the praise, then asked with a spark of excitement, "Dad, do you want to see the second Earth?" Cyrus chuckled, shaking his head. "No, I don't think so. I'm too jealous of them, it only makes me feel depressed."

Ivy laughed softly. "That's exactly how I felt." She turned her gaze from her father to Ethan, her eyes gleaming with playful mischief. "Let's explore our own cities instead. It should be fun."

Cyrus and Ethan exchanged a glance, then both nodded with a smile. "Let's do it," Ethan said, and with that, the three of them set off into the spirit winds, ready to rediscover the forgotten beauty of their own world.

Ethan paused midair, floating in front of Ivy with a thoughtful look. "Do you want to go to the poor side of the city?" he asked.

Ivy frowned gently and shook her head. "No… I don't want to see people's misery today. Let's go to the rich side of the city."

Cyrus and Ethan both nodded in agreement. In an instant, they glided effortlessly through walls, drifting past towering buildings, sleek cars, and the bustling lives of the elite. No doors blocked them, no eyes noticed them, they were spirits, unseen and untethered.

Ivy felt like she was living the impossible, exploring the world with her father by her side, something even her wildest dreams had never granted her.

While Ethan and Cyrus chatted in the background, their voices soft and distant, Ivy floated upward into a dazzling skyscraper. Every floor was like a world of its own, and each unit more magnificent than the last. She moved slowly through a vast corridor, then into one unit, stunning, elegant, flawlessly crafted. Marble floors, golden accents, crystal chandeliers, walls that seemed to breathe art.

Her curiosity deepened. She wanted to see them all, every single unit, every detail, how each space had been prepared and personalized. It felt like stepping into a collection of dreams sculpted into reality.

She floated effortlessly from room to room, marveling at how freely she could move, doing things that, in reality, were impossible. No walls could stop her. No locks, no alarms.

A mischievous thought crossed her mind, and a grin slowly formed on her face. *This is every thief's dream,* she mused. *To slip into the homes of the rich without being seen. To find out exactly where they hide their money, their gold, their precious things… even their security passwords.*

She could see it all, their schedules, when they were home, when they left, especially those long, luxurious vacations. *Just imagine,* she thought, *someone returning to their body with all this information, ready to plan the perfect heist.*

The absurdity of it hit her all at once, and she burst into laughter, the sound echoing through the gilded hallways like wind through crystal.

Something at the far end of the hallway caught Ivy's eye. A strange energy pulsed there, dark, heavy, unnatural. She drifted toward it, curiosity giving way to a creeping unease.

A man stood with his back to her, rigid, unmoving. At his feet, another man crouched on the floor, trembling, his face pale with fear, his wide eyes darting between the figure before him and something behind.

Ivy floated closer, her heart beginning to race. Then she saw them. A woman stood against the wall, shielding a little girl with her body. Tears streamed down her face as she pleaded, her voice shaking. "Please... please, let her live... She's just a child..." The man holding the woman's arms gritted his teeth and snarled, "Shut up, you bitch."

The words struck Ivy like a slap. The air around her grew cold. The beauty of the luxury building vanished in an instant, replaced by something twisted and terrifying hidden within its walls.

The closer Ivy drifted, the clearer the scene became, sharper, heavier, and more horrifying with every step. Armed guards stood like statues in the hallway, their faces expressionless, clutching heavy rifles and watching over the entrance of the unit with mechanical focus. They were there to make sure no one, not even the bravest, dared come close.

Inside the apartment, chaos ruled. Two men were ransacking the place, tearing through drawers, dumping cabinets, slashing open mattresses, ripping cushions apart with savage urgency, as if something precious was hidden deep within the luxury.

The man who stood in front of the trembling figure on the floor radiated command, he was the leader, no doubt. His presence sucked the light from the room. The air around him seemed colder.

Ivy hesitated, her instincts flaring. But then she remembered, they couldn't see her. Not here. Not in this state.

Swallowing her fear, she floated through the wall and into the room. Her gaze fixed on the man standing over the one on the floor. She drifted around to see his face… And when she did, her breath caught. Her body tensed, her soul recoiled. Panic surged through her. She knew that face.

Panic surged through Ivy, and for a moment, she darted back and forth in the air, her thoughts spinning out of control. Her mind was screaming, her instincts telling her to run, yet there was nowhere to run in the spirit world.

Then it hit her again, they couldn't see her.

She forced herself to stop, to breathe, and hovered silently between the leader and the terrified man crumpled on the floor. Her eyes locked onto the man standing tall, commanding the room with cruelty, and slowly, memories pieced themselves together.

I know him…

Her thoughts sharpened. *He's the chief of police. They're supposed to protect people. But as far as I can see, he's doing the opposite. That woman and her daughter, he's letting them be abused. And the man… he's being threatened, tortured right in front of them.*

Then it clicked. "I remember his name now," she whispered, her voice filled with disbelief. "He's Chief Bennett. But… what is he doing here, with this poor family?"

The image shattered everything she thought she knew. The uniform, the title, it meant nothing now. The two men who had been tearing the apartment apart returned to the living room, their faces tense with frustration. They shook their heads at Chief Bennett, a silent message: *Nothing found.*

The woman's voice broke through the silence, raw with fear. She clung to her daughter as tears streamed down her face. "Carl! What do they want? Just give it to them!"

Carl's eyes welled with helplessness. He looked at her, then turned slowly to face Chief Bennett. His voice trembled. "I don't have it. They tricked me… and before I got home, it was gone. They must've stolen it from my car."

He took a shaky breath, his hands raised in a plea. "Please… leave my family out of this. I'll find it, I swear I will."

Every word dripped with desperation. He was cracking under the pressure, his mind spiraling. And still, Chief Bennett said nothing, his eyes cold, unreadable. Chief Bennett stared coldly at Carl, his voice like steel. "I'm sorry, but it's too late. I'll find it anyway… but you're done."

He turned toward the woman and the little girl, his gaze devoid of mercy. Then he gave a chilling command to his right-hand man: "Kill them all." Without a backward glance, he walked out of the room.

The woman screamed and threw herself over her daughter. "Noooooooo! Please!" she cried, her voice breaking with terror. Carl, still on the floor, begged through sobs, "Please, don't hurt them! Take me, kill me, but not my family!"

As his pleas echoed, the Chief returned, stepping back into the room with unsettling calm. "You know what?" he said casually. "It's your lucky day." He drew his gun and glanced at the man holding the mother and child. "Take the girl," he ordered.

The man yanked the girl from her mother's arms. The woman clung to her daughter, screaming, "Leave her alone! Please, she's just a child!" But her cries meant nothing. The man dragged the little girl from the apartment, her mother's wails trailing behind them.

Chief Bennett turned toward the woman. His gun raised slowly. "This is your last chance," he said, staring down at Carl.

"I'll find it for you!" Carl pleaded. "Please, just don't hurt her!" But the Chief's eyes didn't waver. He turned and fired. One shot. The woman collapsed instantly, her body limp, blood spreading beneath her.

Ivy screamed, her voice cracking through the spirit world. "No! No, No!" Chief Bennett didn't react. He looked at his right-hand man and said coldly, "I'll deal with him later." Then he turned and left without another word.

The second man stepped forward, stared down at Carl, and without hesitation, slammed the handle of his gun against Carl's head. Carl dropped instantly, unconscious.

With methodical precision, the man crouched beside him, pried the Chief's gun into Carl's hand, then gently placed a broken vase into the dead woman's fingers, smearing her prints across the sharp edges.

He positioned Carl's limp body just right, twisted the scene into a portrait of domestic violence, of guilt, rage, and chaos. Then, satisfied, he stood, looked around one final time… and disappeared.

The scene was staged perfectly. And Ivy was left there, frozen in horror. A jolt of realization struck Ivy, *the little girl!*

She shot out of the apartment like a streak of light, rushing through the halls, out of the building, and into the street. Her eyes scanned desperately until she spotted them, two black cars parked near the curb. "There they were."

The men were walking toward the vehicles, the little girl between them, her small hand gripped tightly by one of them. Ivy didn't hesitate. In an instant, she phased into the back seat of the first car.

The little girl sat quietly, curled into herself, her eyes wide with fear and brimming with tears. The man beside her leaned in, trying to soften his expression, his voice forced into a gentle tone.

"Don't worry," he said with a fake smile. "You'll be with your parents in no time."

The girl didn't blink. She didn't believe him, not for a second. "I'm Paul," the man continued, still smiling falsely. "Are you Angela?" The little girl gave a timid nod, her expression still frozen in terror. She looked like she was trying to vanish into the seat.

Ivy hovered inches away, her heart pounding with rage and helplessness. *They were going to lie to her, manipulate her, maybe worse.* And yet, in this form, she couldn't touch, couldn't speak, couldn't stop them.

But she *had* to do something. Even if she couldn't stop them now, maybe she could find out where they were taking Angela, what they planned to do to her. Ivy pressed herself deeper into the car, focused, sharp. Her mind raced, but she refused to panic. *Just observe. Just remember.*

She studied each face with precision, etching every detail into her memory, the lines around Paul's mouth when he lied, the cold flatness in the eyes of the man in the front seat, the nervous twitch in the driver's fingers. Every feature, every movement, she locked it away for later. Her heart ached for Angela. The little girl sat silently, trembling, her eyes still full of tears, clutching the edge of the seat like it was the only solid thing left in her world.

The car drove for 45 minutes, winding through quiet roads until it reached a large, secluded house. Tall iron gates, thick hedges, and a long driveway. This wasn't just a home. It was a fortress.

As they pulled up, Paul leaned forward and said, "Call her to come and get the girl."

The man in the passenger seat pulled out his phone without hesitation. After a brief exchange, he hung up and turned back, his voice cold and empty. "She'll be here in five minutes."

Ivy's stomach twisted. *Who was "she"?* What kind of person would take Angela from her mother's arms and become part of this horror?

She didn't have answers, yet. But one thing burned in Ivy's heart like fire: she *would not* leave Angela. Not now. Not ever.

Exactly five minutes later, a woman appeared at the end of the driveway. Middle-aged, with gentle features and a soft presence, she walked toward the car with calm, measured steps. She looked like someone who might bake cookies, not take children. But Ivy had learned not to trust appearances.

When she reached the car, Paul opened the door and gestured toward her. "Angela, this is Tina. Say hi to her."

Angela's terrified eyes shifted to the woman. Something about Tina's calm demeanor made her flinch a little less. Her small voice barely rose above a whisper. "Hello."

Another woman followed behind, much younger, maybe in her twenties. She stepped closer, held out a hand with an awkward smile, and gently scratched her fingertips against Angela's arm, testing her comfort. Angela didn't react.

The young woman softly took Angela's hand, and the two of them walked toward the house. The little girl moved slowly, hesitantly, but not resisting.

Tina remained by the car, waiting for instructions. Paul looked at her and said firmly, "Keep her safe. She's important, until I tell you what to do with her."

Tina didn't blink. Her voice was flat, emotionless. "Alright." She turned and walked away.

Ivy watched, frozen with indecision. *Do I follow the girl? Stay close to her? Or do I follow them, Paul and the others, and find out what this is really about?*

Her eyes shifted from the girl's fragile figure disappearing into the house to the cold men in the front seats. She clenched her jaw.

Until Paul gives her an order, Angela should be safe, she thought. *But I need to know what they're planning. I have to know.*

She turned and looked outside, memorizing the street name, the house number, the shape of the driveway, the iron gate, every detail. Then she stayed. Quiet, invisible, and burning with purpose.

The car began to move, gliding silently down the darkened road. No one spoke. The atmosphere inside was thick, like a sealed room with no air, each man stiff, hollow, like they were just bodies going through motions.

But then Ivy heard it. A voice, soft, trembling, echoed not in the air, but in her mind. *"I don't know if I can do it. I'm scared to say no."* Startled, she turned and focused on the driver. *"I can't,"* the voice whispered again, clearer now, an inner confession.

Ivy's eyes widened. She wasn't just observing, she was hearing his thoughts. His fear. His doubt.

The other two men, however, were eerily still. Their minds were void, silent, blank. Not a flicker of thought, not even a whisper of emotion. They were like statues with beating hearts. *How is that possible?* Ivy wondered, a chill racing down her spine. *They're like machines... or controlled.* But the driver, he was different.

She leaned in closer, her presence wrapping like a soft current around his troubled mind. His knuckles whitened on the steering wheel, his chest rising and falling with short, uneven breaths. Marcus wasn't just driving, he was unraveling.

And Ivy saw it. This wasn't just fear. It was guilt. Desperation. The last threads of a man caught in something far darker than he ever signed up for. She stared at his trembling hands, watching as the shaking worsened, creeping up his arms like a wave of collapse.

The man in the passenger seat finally noticed. He turned his head sharply and asked, "Marcus, what's wrong?" Marcus didn't answer, not with words. But Ivy could hear the storm inside him: *"I should go through the bridge... end it. Kill them... kill myself. I can't take this anymore."*

Ivy's heart jolted. *No.* Angela needed him. *She* needed him. This was the only crack in their wall. And she couldn't let it shatter.

Without hesitation, Ivy reached out and placed her hand gently on Marcus's shoulder. Her fingers passed through, ghost-like, yet something happened.

He inhaled sharply, his grip loosening just slightly. The storm inside him didn't vanish, but it paused, like a trembling chord held in suspension. "I'm fine," he said, his voice low but steady. "Nothing's wrong."

Ivy looked at her hand, glowing faintly with something she didn't understand, some force beyond reason. She'd touched him… and calmed him. In the quiet, she heard his whisper to himself. "Marcus, you are strong. Keep hold of yourself." Ivy knew, in that moment, he hadn't surrendered. And neither would she.

The silence in the car had felt like armor, impenetrable, suffocating. But then, like a crack splitting down the middle of a glass wall, the other man's thoughts surfaced. Ivy heard them clearly, and they chilled her to the core. *"He is trouble. Paul was right. I'll talk to the Chief."* His eyes shifted toward Marcus, narrow and calculating. Ivy's breath caught.

The look he gave Marcus wasn't just suspicious, it was lethal. She felt it, that unspoken decision forming behind those cold eyes. *"They're going to kill him,"* Ivy whispered, trembling.

She floated just inches from Marcus, desperate to shield him, to protect this one thread of humanity in the middle of all this horror. She didn't know how, not yet. But she wouldn't let Marcus be their next victim. Not when he was the only one who could still choose *not* to be a monster.

Ivy turned her eyes and saw Ethan and her father standing beside her. "What are you doing here, Ivy?" Ethan asked, his voice laced with concern, while her father's eyes mirrored the same confusion.

"I need to save a little girl named Angela," she replied firmly.

"Who is the little girl? And why is she your concern?" Cyrus asked, his brow furrowed. Ivy didn't answer right away; she was too distracted, her mind tuned in to Paul and the other two men's thoughts. She stared hard at Paul before finally speaking.

"They want something from her father, who's innocent, I saw it in his mind. But they killed her mother and staged it to look like he did it. Now they've taken the girl to force him to talk."

Her words came fast, tangled and heavy, leaving both Cyrus and Ethan stunned. "What???" they said in unison, confusion and disbelief flashing across their faces.

"Ivy, why is this any of your concern?" her father asked, pointing at her with urgency. She looked at him, her mind momentarily blank, then answered, her voice trembling with conviction.

"What are you talking about, Dad? She's being held captive, and they might torture her in front of her father to break him." Her gaze shifted from Cyrus to Ethan, eyes blazing with purpose. "She needs help. And I think… that's why I'm here. It's directed at me, this purpose, this moment. I'm here to save her. Otherwise… why else would I be there at all?"

Cyrus panicked and pulled her close, his voice sharp with fear. "Ivy, these people are dangerous. You can't get involved. They'll kill anyone who stands in the way of their twisted games."

Ethan nodded, his expression grave. "He's right, Ivy. Don't get tangled up with them. These aren't just criminals, they're ruthless. If they even suspect you know something, they won't hesitate to kill you."

Ivy looked at her father and said, "I know that, I saw with my own eyes how Chief heartlessly killed her mother in front of her husband and kidnapped his daughter to force him to talk. I know, but she is in trouble and I'm the only one who can help her."

Cyrus saw the resolve in her eyes and grew even more anxious. "But Ivy," he said, his voice trembling, "you're putting Liam in danger, your friends too. Anyone close to you could get hurt." Ethan continued nodding in agreement, silent but supportive of Cyrus' concern.

Ivy's face twisted with guilt and determination. "I know, Dad. That's why I need a plan. I can't get involved physically, I have to find another way." Ethan finally spoke, gently but firmly. "Then let's think it through. Sleep on it. We'll meet tomorrow and figure something out."

Ivy shook her head, frustration flashing in her eyes. "We don't have that kind of time. If we wait, it might already be too late." Cyrus jumped on her last words, his brows furrowed. "You said Chief? Who is he?"

"Chief Bennett," Ivy replied without hesitation. "I saw him. He shot that innocent woman. He's part of all this."

Cyrus recoiled in disbelief. "Chief of the police department? Are you serious? Ivy, there's absolutely nothing you can do. Please, be wiser, walk away from this." But Ivy had reached her breaking point. Her voice trembled as she looked straight into her father's eyes.

"Dad, we're talking about a six-year-old girl, just a child, who might be tortured or even killed. Where's the justice in that?" Her voice cracked with emotion. "How can I go home, smile, and pretend life is okay while that little girl suffers? How?"

Alina appeared at the door and said brightly, "Hello." No one responded. The tension in there was too thick to cut through. She glanced around, puzzled. "Hey... what's going on?" Ethan turned to her with a strained smile. "Nothing much, just Ivy playing Sherlock Holmes."

Alina blinked. "What?" In a rush, Ethan filled her in, summarizing everything in under a minute. She looked from one face to the next, absorbing the weight of what had been said. Then, with calm resolve, she nodded. "She's right. We have to do something about that little girl. "Ethan, we did worse than that."

Ethan turned to Alina, his voice low with concern. "She's not strong enough right now. I don't know if she's ready for this kind of rescue."

Then Alina turned to Ivy and asked firmly, "Do you have a plan?"

Ivy was still lost in thought when the car began to slow in front of a looming building. Suddenly, Paul's phone rang. He answered without a word, only listening. A cold voice came through the line, "Carl is in custody. Get ready for the investigation." The call ended abruptly. Everyone in the car had heard it.

Paul turned to Marcus, his expression unreadable. "I'll be back in fifteen minutes. Wait here." Marcus gave a silent nod, his grip tightening slightly on the wheel.

Alina's voice was urgent with concern. "Ivy, you have to leave now. Class will be over in fifteen minutes, and if you're not back, if your body stays unresponsive, they'll know something's wrong."

Ivy's face fell, her frustration growing. "But I have to stay. I need to find out what's going on." Ethan stepped forward calmly. "I'll stay. I'll follow them and see where they go." Cyrus nodded, aligning with her determination. "Just tell me where the little girl is, and I'll get every bit of information you need."

Alina smiled gently and turned to Ivy. "See? You've got your own team of investigators now." Ivy looked around at all of them, her heart full of gratitude. She took her father's hand and said softly, "I'll show you where the little girl is." Then, with a final glance at Ethan and Alina, she and Cyrus disappeared.

Ivy was home, but her mind refused to rest. Thoughts of Angela kept circling like a storm. *Where is she? Is she scared? Hurt?* The questions gnawed at her. She closed her eyes and tried to recall the street name.

"Crank Raw…" she whispered. A jolt of uncertainty ran through her. "No, no, no. That's not it." She sprang to her laptop, hands trembling as she typed furiously, trying every variation of street names she could remember. Nothing. Nothing made sense.

Her breath quickened. Her heart pounded. The screen blurred as frustration clawed at her. "Angela," she whispered, her voice breaking, "I have to find you…"

It was past midnight, and Ivy's body refused to surrender to sleep. Rest was a stranger. She reached for her phone to make a call, then hesitated. *She's probably still there with Ethan and my dad. She won't answer.*

With a quiet sigh, she set the phone down and lay back on her bed, sinking deep into her thoughts. She needed a plan. Not a reckless idea, something solid, smart, something that could outwit professionals. These people weren't just dangerous. They were trained, calculated, and cruel.

"A plan," she whispered into the darkness, her fingers clutching the edge of her blanket. *A plan… God, help me. I have to do something. If You placed me on this path… then You have to help me walk it, too.*

She opened her eyes, and as if by magic, it was morning. No memory of falling asleep, just a quiet shift from darkness to daylight. She got ready mechanically, but her thoughts never stopped. Angela. Carl. The fear. The urgency.

Ethan and Dad should have more info, she told herself. *Unless I go back there, I'll never find out where Angela or Carl are.*

The whole day passed in a blur. She went through the motions, but her mind was far away. Vincent noticed. He stepped quietly into her office, and Ivy looked up, startled. "What's up, Vincent?" He studied her, concern lining his face. "Are you okay today? You don't seem like yourself." Ivy blinked, thrown by the question. "Yes… I'm alright. Why?"

Vincent hesitated, searching her face. "Because… you came to my office three times. Opened the door. Didn't say a word, then just walked away." He paused, his voice softer. "What's going on, Ivy? How can I help you?"

Ivy saw the opening, an unexpected chance. Maybe time away would help her think, help her act. She looked at Vincent, her expression softening into something serious and sincere. "Nothing serious," she said quietly. "It's just… when it gets close to the anniversary of my dad's death, it hits me harder than I expect." She paused, her voice growing heavier. "This Wednesday will be one year since he passed away."

Vincent's expression softened, concern etched deeply in his features. "How can I help you? Do you want to take some time off, step away, calm your mind, maybe rest a little?" Ivy nodded slowly, her voice gentle. "If that's okay with you… it would be good." Vincent smiled warmly and gently nodded.

"Just make sure to see me before you go," he said.

"I will. Thanks," Ivy replied softly.

Later, as Emma and Ivy stepped out of the building together, the sun low and golden, Emma glanced over and asked, "What happened? Why were you in Vincent's office?" Ivy offered a small smile. "I just needed some time off. To be by myself for a little while."

She paused, her voice lowering with emotion. "In a few days, it'll be one year since my dad passed away. I know I can still see him, in a different way, but it's not the same. I miss the little things. Having breakfast together… going places. Just… being with him." She left out everything about Angela. The crime. The danger. Emma didn't need to be dragged into it. Not now. Ivy knew she had to move carefully.

"Are you still willing to go for yoga?" Emma asked gently, concern in her eyes. "Yes," Ivy replied with a reassuring smile. "Nothing's changed. I just want to be home a little more often."

Emma nodded slowly. "You probably want to go to the other side… be with your dad. If that's okay, I can come stay with you. Just to make sure you'll be fine." Ivy felt the care behind her words, the quiet worry Emma was trying to hide. She appreciated it. Truly.

"That's up to you," Ivy said kindly. "But I really don't need help. You'd be alone all day, and honestly, it'd be boring for you. Besides," she added with a smile. "Alina always calls afterward to make sure I got back safely." Emma smiled back, but the worry didn't fully leave her eyes.

Ivy got home, took a shower, and had her dinner, making sure her body had enough energy to sustain her in the other realm. She sat on her bed, eyes heavy with thought, searching for a way to enter the building that had taken Angela, perhaps a daycare center in disguise, and in that eerie place, she believed Tina held the key.

The name of the street echoed in her mind like a riddle, strange and slippery. She opened her laptop and began scouring the web, but the name was too odd, too elusive. Nothing made sense. Frustrated and restless, she lay back and closed her eyes, focusing hard.

"IVY?" Ethan's voice cut through the silence, loud, clear, unmistakable. She opened her eyes and smiled. "What's new? Did you find out about Carl?" Her gaze darted around, hopeful. But her father wasn't there. "Where is my dad?"

Cyrus smiled and said, "I'm here, sweetheart." Ivy's face lit up. "Good to see you again, Dad." Cyrus nodded gently, then spoke with quiet urgency. "Ivy, they've kept Carl locked in a room in the basement of a building. You were right, he truly doesn't know anything about the missing packages. But they won't believe him, simply because he was in charge. And we can't extract any information from his mind about that time, because there's nothing there to find."

"And I searched the place where Angela," Ethan said. "She's in a room, unharmed. They're taking care of her, but… there's something off about the way they're acting. It doesn't feel right."

Ivy listened intently to both of them, her mind racing. Then she spoke, her voice firm. "We have to act fast. They might be keeping Angela safe for now, but only until they give up on Carl. If they decide to make him talk, they'll use her. We need to find out who's behind this, and figure out how to save both Angela and Carl before it's too late."

She said, "I have to go to that place, or daycare, whatever it is. I need to find out more about Tina and the others."

Ethan gave a crooked smile. "I doubt you'll get anything useful out of them. They're… strange. It's like their minds aren't even operating in real time. Just robotic responses, nothing human about the way they think."

Ivy listened, then nodded with quiet resolve. "That's alright. I still have to try. I need to see it for myself."

Cyrus looked at her with quiet pride. "Ivy, please, don't do anything reckless. Be very careful. I think I might be able to do something to help with this situation. Just give me a little time, and I'll be back soon." With that, he vanished into the mist.

Ivy turned to Ethan. "Would you please go to Carl and stay with him? If anything changes, let me know right away." Ethan gave a respectful nod before he, too, disappeared into the shadows.

Like the blink of an eye, Ivy found herself beside Angela. The little girl was sitting quietly on a tiny bed, her posture still, her face innocent and lost in thought. Ivy glanced around the room. "God, I love this realm," she whispered to herself. "No traffic, no waiting, and in a heartbeat, I'm here."

The room was simple, scattered with toys, but Angela showed no interest in any of them. Her stillness spoke louder than words. Ivy gently reached out with her mind, tuning into Angela's thoughts.

Mommy! Daddy! I'm scared. Why aren't you coming to pick me up?

The ache in those words pierced Ivy's heart. She sat beside Angela and wrapped her arms around her. Instantly, she felt the child's body ease, the fear melting ever so slightly into calm. "I'm here now," Ivy murmured softly. "And I promise, I won't let anything happen to you."

For a moment, Ivy felt Angela's eyes lock with hers, deep, innocent, and searching. Then, to her surprise, Angela smiled. A soft, genuine smile that lit up her little face. Ivy held her breath, unsure if the girl could truly see her. But a flicker of hope sparked in Ivy's chest when Angela stood and walked over to pick up a doll from the floor. She exhaled quietly, feeling a little more at ease. Ivy kept watching her as she turned away, offering a faint smile over her shoulder. "Thanks," she said softly. Ivy rose to her feet, unsure whether Angela had actually seen heror if it had all been just a coincidence.

Slipping out into the hallway, Ivy moved silently past the rooms, her senses alert. It wasn't long before she spotted Tina. She was hunched over a desk, rifling through files with practiced ease. Ivy stepped closer and glanced at the file Tina was examining. It wasn't Angela's. It belonged to someone else entirely.

Ivy turned to leave, but then Tina spoke in her mind, unaware of her presence. "I hope they find whatever it is from her father, because I've already lined up a great couple to adopt her, and the money? Wow, amazing. But if the father won't talk... well, it would be such a shame to lose her." Ivy froze. A chill ran down her spine.

She tried to leave the room when the phone rang. Tina picked it up and answered briskly, "Haven-reach Institute, how may I help you?"

Ivy froze in place, whispering to herself, "Havenreach Institute… okay." She held her breath, listening closely.

Tina continued, her tone smooth and professional. "Yes, that's correct. We lost one of our beloved nannies last week, and we urgently need a replacement. You can send your resume to havenreachinstitute.com, and we'll take it from there." A short pause followed. "Yes, the deadline would be next Friday. Have a good day."

As she hung up, Tina turned toward the window, her expression unreadable. "Poor Gloria," she murmured. "She was one of the good ones. How can I replace her? I need someone as obedient as Gloria." Ivy's eyes gleamed with sudden hope. Her heart raced. This might be the way in.

She had found everything she needed here, and with a swish, she was beside Ethan. He looked tense. "Paul is coming to speak with Carl," he told her.

Ivy's heart dropped. Fear tightened in her chest; she didn't know what Paul might do. As her thoughts raced, her focus locked on him, and just like that, she was there, standing beside Paul.

He was pacing, visibly agitated, his jaw clenched and his eyes sharp with frustration. Something was off. He looked… nervous. The phone on his desk rang, slicing through the silence. Paul froze, staring at it as though it were a venomous snake. After a beat, he picked up the receiver with visible reluctance.

"Hello, Paul Madison speaking." Chief Bennett's voice came crisply from the other end. "Paul, it's Simon. Come to my office." Without missing a beat, Paul responded, "Yes, I'm on my way." He hung up quickly, the tension in his face deepening. Ivy watched him, the unease inside her growing darker.

He started walking and left the room. In the hallway, his thoughts spiraled, jumping chaotically from one incident to the next.

"Marcus is a problem. He saw us taking the packages. He was supposed to be locked away, damn stupid. I'll kill him." His fists clenched as he walked faster, his face dark with fury. *"Carl... I'll make him confess. A false confession to protect his daughter. He has no choice. He'll take the fall, and then I'll kill them both."*

Ivy stood frozen in place, her breath caught in her throat. She couldn't believe what she was hearing. Carl and Marcus, both innocent. And Angela's mother... she had lost her life for nothing.

Ivy went to Chief Bennett's office and waited in silence, her presence invisible but alert. A moment later, Paul walked in, tension radiating off him. Chief Bennett didn't waste time, he pointed at Paul sharply.

"Did you get anything out of him? We're dealing with Dante *'Black Veil'* Morado. And he's not going to wait for us to piece together the truth about the packages. We need an answer, now. I'm waiting for his call. And you know he only gives one chance. After that… there's nothing."

Dante gave a hollow, unsettling laugh. "One hundred and ten billion dollars are ready for you." Then, without another word, he hung up. Silence filled the room, heavy, dangerous. Ivy's heart pounded. The stakes were far higher than she had imagined.

She moved back to Ethan in an instant, her mind still reeling. Without wasting a second, she told him everything, what she saw, what she heard, every word that passed between Chief Bennett and Paul, and the chilling call from Dante "Black Veil" Morado.

Ivy turned to Ethan, her voice firm and unwavering. "I have to go. I have a lot to do. But please, keep an eye on them and keep me posted however you can."

Ethan blinked, caught off guard by the sudden determination in her tone. "What are you planning to do?"

She glanced at him, then at Carl in the distance, and finally answered, "I need a fake ID. I'm going to apply for a job at the place where they're keeping Angela. I'm getting her out, before they even think about hurting her."

Ethan's expression darkened. He shook his head. "Ivy, it's too dangerous. Don't do that."

Ivy met his eyes, her voice steady and resolute. "Too dangerous? A five-year-old girl is about to be sacrificed for some greedy bastards chasing money. I'm asking God to help me. If I survive, I'll live. If I don't… at least I'll have done something that mattered. I'll go with my dad, knowing I tried to save a life."

She paused. "If you want to help me, I'll be grateful. But I won't push you. It's your choice." She gave Ethan one last look, gentle, but full of fire, then turned and walked away.

It was 4 in the morning. Ivy sat wide awake, her mind racing, trying to figure out how to get a fake ID. Then it struck her, *the name of the place*. She grabbed her laptop, opened it, and typed in: *Haven Reach Institute*. She hit Enter.

Within seconds, a flood of information appeared on the screen. The address stood out immediately: **25 Crooked Lantern**. She clicked through the site, searching for the *Careers* section, and there it was. A position was open. Pages filled with glossy images, information about adoption, sponsorship, and more scrolled in front of her eyes. She started printing everything she could.

Suddenly, the phone rang, startling her so much she nearly dropped the laptop. She looked at the screen. *Private number.*

She ignored it. It rang again. And again.

Finally, she exhaled sharply and answered, her voice edgy. "Who is it? Who are you, and why are you calling at this time?" A voice, warm and clear, came through the speaker, and Ivy froze. "Ivy, it's me… Ethan." Her breath caught. It was the first time she'd ever heard his voice outside the other realm.

"Ethan?" she whispered. "Yes," he said gently. "I called you because you said you needed a fake ID, and I know someone who can help. I knew I couldn't stop you… but at least I can help."

Ivy's throat tightened, her voice turning tender. "Thank you, Ethan. And… I'm sorry I yelled at you. I really appreciate this."

She hesitated, then asked quietly, "So… you're really alive?"

Ethan replied with a smile she could hear. "Of course I am. I told you that."

Another pause. Then softly, "Is Ethan your real name?"

He gave a small chuckle. "Yes, it is."

"I already talked to the guy; he's expecting your call. His name is Silas Quade. Quiet, nerdy, and way too good at forgery, exactly what you're looking for. This is his number: 647-555-2755, for now. Call him right away."

Ivy jotted down the information, nodding. "I will. But why did you say this number is his number *for now*?"

Ethan hesitated, then said, "Because his number changes every time he gives it out. Each one works only once."

"Got it," Ivy said. "Thanks, Ethan."

Just before he hung up, he added, "Keep me posted, and I'll see you at our usual."

Ivy chuckled. "Okay. I like it when you call it our usual, but how can I do that? I only see you at our usual."

There was a pause, then he said, "You can reach me at this website, www.QuantumCrumbs.com"

They both laughed softly before the line went silent. She stared at her writing for a moment, then dialed the number. After two rings, a voice answered, calm and clear. "Hi, Ivy."

She froze, a flicker of panic tightening her chest. "How do you know it's me? Did Ethan tell you that?" Silas chuckled softly. "Yeah. He only mentioned your name and that you need a fake number."

The tension in her chest eased. She'd panicked for nothing. "So," Silas continued, his tone curious but unhurried, "how can I help you?"

"I need a first and last name. Also, I need some documents to go with it. Can you handle that?" Silas didn't hesitate. "I can do more than that. But I'll need some details, like what it's for. I've got a lot of experience, and depending on the purpose, you might need extra or specific documents. I can help you figure that out."

"I can't tell you that. It's dangerous, and I don't want to drag you into it," Ivy whispered. Silas let out a soft chuckle, then replied, "In that case, I'm probably the only one you can trust. I can get you whatever you're looking for, and more. I'm able to do exclusive research on anything you've got in mind."

He paused, his voice steady and confident. "So… how can I help you?"

She hesitated, torn between doubt and trust. But Ethan had introduced him, and Ethan already knew her plan. Her voice softened. "I'm planning to get hired at a place called Haven Reach Institute. I need something that proves I'm the right person, something that makes them hire me."

Silas didn't respond. The silence stretched long enough that Ivy glanced at her phone. "Hello? Are you still there?"

Finally, Silas spoke, his tone calm and focused. "Yeah, I'm here. Give me twenty minutes, I'll find out exactly what they're looking for. I'll call you back. Please make sure you're available."

Ivy nodded instinctively. "Okay. But… you *will* call, right?"

"Of course," Silas said simply. "This is my job." Then the line went dead.

Time dragged unbearably for Ivy. Every second felt like an hour. She kept checking the clock; only a minute had passed. The wait gnawed at her nerves, stretching endlessly. She stared at her phone, willing it to ring, when suddenly, Ethan appeared.

Her eyes widened in shock. "Hey! What are you doing here? How am   I   able   to   see   you   now?"

Ethan smiled with quiet certainty. "You still haven't realized how effortlessly and how fast you move between realms. Ivy, you're outside your body. You're incredible at this. It's like second nature to you."

Ivy looked around, feeling an odd sense of calm wash over her. "Is my father back?"

Ethan shook his head. "No, but he said he might be able to do something, remember?"

She nodded slowly. "Yes. And when he says he can do something… it usually means it's already a fact." She glanced around again, then her expression shifted. "Oh no! I have to go back. Your friend is going to call me, so I have to be there." Before Ethan could respond, she vanished in a blink. She checked the time again; only twenty-five minutes had passed. Her chest tightened with unease. The anxiety was too much. She couldn't sit still. Then, suddenly, the phone rang. She didn't even know how her hand moved so fast; she snatched it up and answered breathlessly, "Hello?" A soft, familiar voice came through. "Hi Ivy, I was worried about you, so I thought I'd call and see how you're doing."

Ivy's mind was spinning elsewhere. "Emma? Is it you?"

"Yes, it's me," Emma replied cheerfully. "How do you do?"

Ivy's eyes were glued to the clock, twenty minutes, exactly. "Emma, I'm waiting for an important call. I'll call you later, I really have to go."

Emma's voice was still warm as she said, "No prob..." but Ivy had already hung up.

She looked frustrated now, her brows furrowed. "It's almost half an hour… what's taking him so long?"

She didn't even finish the thought when the phone rang. Ivy grabbed it instantly. "Hi."

Silas's voice came through, calm but serious. "Hi. Sorry for the delay. It was harder than I expected. Did you know they're a branch of the CIA?"

Ivy's stomach twisted. "What??"

"I know," Silas said gently. "It's a lot to take in. But the real question is, why do you want to join an organization like that?"

Ivy's thoughts scattered. "Are you sure about that? How do you know?"

Silas's voice tightened, more certain now. He could tell she truly didn't know. "So you didn't know. That's what I was afraid of." He paused, then added, "Is this new information enough to make you walk away from them? I really hope the answer is yes."

"I don't want to work for them. Would you please just prepare the paperwork for me?" She paused, then added, "By the way, how much do you charge?"

Silas was silent for a moment. Then he asked, "If you don't want to work for them, why are you trying to get hired?" A beat passed. "And my price is $2, 000, cash."

Ivy said nothing. She couldn't tell him the truth, couldn't risk exposing Angela or endangering her. "Okay," she finally said. "When can I get the documents? And how will you get them to me?"

Silas didn't answer right away. When he did, his voice was unusually calm. "They've already chosen someone, a girl named Harriet. But I can change that. I can discredit her with a false accusation and push your resume to the top."

A chill ran through Ivy, and a cold sweat broke across her skin. "And for that... how much extra do you expect?"

Silas gave a quiet chuckle. "How much is too much to you? Because they are very dangerous people."

Ivy stared at the window, then answered, "I'll pay whatever is your price."

Silas gave a quiet chuckle. "No extra. I'm just curious, and I want to help. You sound honest, and I get the feeling you need someone who understands these kinds of movesand knows exactly how to pull them off."

"What's your reason for helping me?" Ivy asked, her voice laced with suspicion. "You don't even know why I'm doing this. But you *do* know these people are dangerous. So why?"

Silas was silent for a moment. Then, his voice came low and steady. "That's exactly the reason. I *do* know them. And I can get anything I need from them without ever standing in front of them."

He paused, then added, "But *you*... you have no experience. None. And you're about to do something risky, something that could destroy you if you're not careful. You need me, Ivy. Because when it comes to them... I'm not just prepared. I'm a threat."

Ivy was caught off guard by his answer. She still couldn't tell if he genuinely wanted to help or if he was just playing along to satisfy his own curiosity. "Okay," she said cautiously. "Are you actually able to get me hired? I just need to get inside for a couple of days, then I'll vanish without a trace. Can you make that happen?"

"That's what I do," Silas replied smoothly. "Once everything's ready, I'll call you with a location. Be ready. Wait for my call." A nervous smile touched Ivy's lips, though a flicker of fear still lingered in her chest.

"How long will it take? Should I expect your call today, or… sometime later?"

Silas let out a loud laugh. "You're good. I like that. Takes guts to pull something like this off, and you clearly have a reason strong enough to risk everything. I respect that. Wait for my call this afternoon."

Ivy felt a weight lift. For the first time, she was genuinely glad to have someone like him on her side. For reasons she couldn't quite explain, she trusted him. "Okay. I'll wait for your call." The line went dead. She picked up her phone and dialed Emma's number, but it went straight to voicemail. She left a quick message, "Hey Emma, sorry I had to cut you off so quickly earlier. I'll let you know as soon as I'm able to head to Alina's office. Talk to you later."

CHAPTER FIVE – No Way Back

By three-thirty, Ivy received the call from Silas. Her hands trembled, she knew that once she had the documents, there would be no turning back.

"I've prepared all the necessary papers you might need in case you get hired," Silas said calmly. "It's three thirty-five now. I can meet you at four o'clock at Fairview Mall—Don Mills and Sheppard. Do you know the location?"

Ivy listened intently, not wanting to miss a single detail. "Yes, I know it. I'll see you there." Silas's tone shifted, firmer now. "You must come alone. If I see anyone else with you, I'm gone, disappeared for good."

"No, please. I'll come alone, I promise. Don't worry," Ivy replied, her voice tight with nerves. "I'll see you there at four."

Immediately, she got dressed and rushed out the door. The traffic was brutal, cars crawling like snails, and her navigation system projected an arrival time of ten after four.

Stress tightened her chest. She didn't have Silas's number, not even Ethan's, to let them know she was running late. There was nothing she could do but keep going and hope—hope that he would wait.

It was four fifteen when she finally arrived at the meeting spot. Her heart pounded with anxiety. She was late, and she had no idea what Silas even looked like. She wandered through the mall, passing the same stores again and again, eyes scanning every face. Nothing. No sign of him.

Frustrated and uneasy, she sank onto a bench, disappointment gnawing at her. Minutes dragged by. At four thirty, she stood up, ready to leave. Just as she turned toward the exit, a hand suddenly slipped into hers.

"Keep walking," a voice said quietly. Ivy froze, she recognized the voice. It was Silas. She opened her mouth to explain, "I'm sorry, the traffic was—"

But he cut her off calmly. "Listen. The traffic doesn't matter. I knew you'd be late. But I needed time to make sure you came alone."

Ivy blinked in confusion. "You mean… you were behind my car the whole time?" Silas's voice stayed cool and steady. "Yes. Like I said, I needed to be sure."

Ivy looked both frustrated and understanding. She nodded slowly. "So… I was worried sick for nothing?" Silas gave a faint smile. "It wasn't for nothing. There was something. That's why you're on this journey because deep down, you know there's a reason you had to be."

Ivy kept staring at him, confused, unsure what to ask or say next. Silas didn't wait. "Let's get back to business. Don't ask me anything until I'm done. Are you with me?" Ivy gave a small smile and nodded.

"This organization," he began, his voice low and firm, "is the dark side of the CIA." Ivy's eyes widened, and she couldn't help but blurt out, "The CIA has a darker side? How dark can they go?"

Silas stopped walking and turned to face her, staring in silence. His expression didn't change. Ivy immediately realized her mistake. "Sorry," she said quickly. "I know I should've been listening. It won't happen again. I promise."

Still, Silas said nothing for a few seconds. His stare remained fixed, unreadable. Then, finally, he spoke. "If it happens again, I walk and you're on your own." Ivy nodded, serious now. She raised her right hand. "Promise."

"As I said." He looked directly into Ivy's eyes, watching carefully to see if she would interrupt again. When she stayed silent, he continued after two seconds.

"This organization is the dark side of the CIA. They work with the most dangerous criminals, using them to solve problems and secure their own interests for the future. They operate without hesitation. If someone is seen as a problem, they remove them. They vanish without a trace. It doesn't matter if that 'problem' is an eighty-year-old grandmother... or a four-year-old child."

He paused, letting the weight of his words settle into the silence. "Any questions before I move on to the next part?" Ivy shook her head slowly, no.

"When you step inside that place, whatever your reason is, you've got 48 hours. That's it. Forty-eight hours to find whatever you're after and get out before they trace you." His voice was firm, deliberate.

"They don't stop. They'll search, and they'll keep searching, every single day. Whatever you touch, they'll lift your fingerprints. They'll find you. They'll know what kind of cologne your neighbor wears, or what breed of dog your father's uncle once had."

He glanced at Ivy again. This time, she was fully focused, her eyes locked on his. No questions, just quiet understanding. She nodded once more. "No."

Silas reached into his backpack and pulled out a small black box. He held it in front of her, then opened it. Inside were ten translucent fingertip covers. He took one, gently grasped her hand, and slid it over her finger. It melded seamlessly with her skin, almost invisible, as if it had never been there.

"While you're inside, you must wear all of them, on every finger," he instructed. "These will mask your fingerprints and protect your identity. I've done my best to make them undetectable."

He pulled out a folder and handed it to her. "I created a complete identity for you. Social media profiles, a SIN number, a birth certificate, all under your alias. Your knowledge, job history, and personal background are all documented in this book. As soon as you get home, you must study it. Memorize it like it's your own life."

Silas's eyes narrowed slightly. "They'll call you tomorrow for an interview. You have to know this identity inside and out. You must answer with absolute confidence, no hesitation."

He paused, then reached into his bag again, pulling out a sleek, metallic case. He opened it to reveal a nearly invisible earpiece, small enough to miss unless you were looking for it.

"You see this?" he said. "This goes in your ear. I'll be listening in. If they ask you something that's not in the book, I'll guide you. But you must stay calm. No panic. No mistakes."

His eyes locked onto hers, steady and unblinking. He needed to be certain she was ready. "Are you absolutely sure you still want to go through with this?"

Ivy didn't hesitate. Her voice was firm. "Yes. I have to. There's a four-year-old girl whose life is in danger. I know they're planning to make her disappear."

Silas nodded slowly. "I know. Ethan told me everything. That's why we're in this, and why we're helping you, because this is what we do." Ivy's eyes widened in disbelief. "You mean… you knew?"

Silas met her gaze with quiet certainty. "Yes. That's why we've prepared all of this. Not just to get you in, but to make sure you come back." He extended his hand, his expression serious. "Ivy, please… be very careful. And come back safe."

Ivy smiled softly and took his hand. They shook firmly, an unspoken promise passing between them, then turned and went their separate ways. She glanced back for one last look. But he was already gone.

Ivy arrived home and immediately tore open the package. Inside was a cellphone and a birth certificate, her new identity.

"Beatrice Tumbleway?" she read aloud, lifting an eyebrow in disbelief. Taped to the phone was a small note in crisp handwriting, **"Do not use this cellphone for personal matters. It will be tracked once you're hired. This is part of your cover."**

Beneath the note was an address—an apartment she was supposed to have lived in for the past ten years. The message continued, **"Go there immediately—before they contact you. Everything has been arranged. Use the key inside the envelope."**

Ivy opened the side of the envelope and felt the cold metal of a key slip into her fingers. This was real. It had already begun. She kept digging. According to the documents, Beatrice was the manager of a bustling daycare center overseeing 250 children. She was also listed as a survivor of a bombing attack in New York City, a detail meant to add depth, maybe even sympathy, to her profile.

There was an overwhelming amount of information to memorize, including employment history, medical records, travel logs, volunteer work, and even favorite books and childhood memories.

She opened the social media accounts. Dozens of photos filled the profiles, vacation snapshots, smiling group photos at daycare events, selfies in various cafes. They looked just enough like her to pass... but she knew they weren't her. It was unsettling. Like staring into a life she'd never lived.

She stood up and, as quickly as she could, gathered everything she might need for at least three days. With her bag slung over her shoulder, she rushed out the door and headed toward her car.

Just as she reached it, a loud honk startled her. She turned, and there was Silas, leaning against an old, beat-up car that looked like it had survived a dozen lives.

She smiled. "What are you doing here?"

Silas grinned back. "Well, you could take your own car, a taxi, or public transit. But if you do, they'll trace where you came from. I'll drive you there instead."

Ivy laughed. "And you're not afraid of getting caught?"

He shrugged, his grin widening. "Who's getting caught? This isn't even my car. I don't know whose it is."

She shook her head, smiling. "You're unbelievable."

Silas's smile faded into something more serious, more certain. "That's what I am. Unbelievable." Silas drove Ivy to her temporary apartment and left without a word.

She stepped inside and found a modest, clean space—nothing fancy, but perfectly livable. She didn't mind it. It felt detached from everything else in her life, which was exactly what she needed.

She unpacked quickly, fully aware that everything she brought would be left behind. She had no intention of taking any of it with her when this was over. Opening the closet, she paused—it was huge. A walk-in, lined with dresses and clothes in her exact size. She smiled and leaned back slightly. "This is amazing. How did he pull that off?"

Back at her place, she had already left a note on the fridge for Liam: *"Gone for a week—just need to clear my head and refresh my memory. Don't worry."* She'd told Emma the same. Her personal cellphone remained at home, untouched.

Now, with a steaming cup of coffee in hand, she sat on the small balcony, legs tucked under her, and watched the city breathe.

It felt less like preparation for a mission… and more like the beginning of a quiet, personal journey. Like traveling, only this time, to a version of herself she'd never met.

She opened the fridge and, to her surprise, found it fully stocked. She made herself a vegetable omelet for dinner and savored it on the balcony, it was a quiet pleasure. The evening air was gentle, and she felt at peace. She stayed there until sundown, soaking in every moment. She had no idea how long she would have to wait for the call, but all she could do was wait. She hoped it would end soon so she could save Angela.

The sky was adorned with stars, and she couldn't take her eyes off it. It was magnificent, breathtaking, just to gaze upon them. In front of the building stretched a vast green space, like a sprawling park or untouched wilderness, making the place feel even more magical. She found herself wondering who lived here and how they had discovered such a hidden gem. At last, she decided to go to bed and prepare for tomorrow.

In the morning, she woke up feeling fresh and alert. She had never slept so peacefully before, it was deeply refreshing, and for the first time in a long while, she felt truly alive. Not since her father passed away had she felt this safe. *Last night was like a magical dream... I don't think I'll ever forget this place,* she thought.

With that lingering warmth in her mind, she took a shower, prepared her breakfast, and set everything out on the balcony. As she returned for her freshly brewed coffee, a sudden ringtone startled her. She didn't recognize it, but followed the sound until she found the phone.

In an instant, everything came rushing back, why she was in that apartment in the first place. She had become so relaxed, she'd nearly forgotten the plan. Quickly, she searched for the earpiece, placed it in her ear, and answered the call, switching it to speaker.

"Good morning, Mrs. Tumbleway?" said the voice on the other end. She recognized it instantly. It was Tina, the woman who had taken Angela from Paul. Without hesitation, Ivy responded, keeping her tone calm and composed.

"Good morning. May I ask who I'm speaking to?" she said in a polished, professional voice. Silas's voice came through the earpiece, steady and encouraging. "That's great. Your tone is perfect. Keep it just like that."

"Mrs. Tumbleway, my name is Tina Greenwood. I'm calling from Haven Reach Institute, a child adoption agency. I recently realized I had overlooked your resume, but by some miracle, I came across it yesterday. Your qualifications are truly impressive, and for that reason, I'd like to invite you for an interview today at 2:00 p.m. Are you available?"

Silas's voice came through the earpiece, calm and instructive. "Tell her just a second, you need to check your calendar first. Then accept it." Ivy nodded subtly and replied, "Yes, Mrs. Greenwood. May I ask for a moment to check my appointments? I wasn't expecting anything today."

"There would be no problem," Tina replied politely. Within half a minute, Ivy responded, "Mrs. Greenwood, I'd be more than happy to meet with you today. Could you please provide me with the address? Thank you."

Tina's voice brightened. "I'll send the address to your email shortly. It was a pleasure speaking with you. See you at 2:00 o'clock. Good day." Ivy thanked her, and the line went dead.

Silas said, "Don't rush. You need to look calm, cool, and completely organized. Ivy, remember, every single time before you leave the apartment, you must wipe down everything you've touched and use the fingerprint tips to replace any trace with those prints. They have your address now, and there's a ninety percent chance they'll come and inspect the place. It's better if you wear the finger tips at all times."

"Okay, I'll do that," Ivy replied. "May I ask, who lived here before?" But Silas was gone. The earpiece fell silent.

Without another word, Ivy got to work. She carefully wiped down every surface she had touched with a clean tissue. Then, wearing the artificial fingertip covers, she methodically re-touched the coffee pot, the doorknob, the bed frame, the table and chair on the balcony, the balcony door, everywhere she could remember laying her fingers. She didn't remove the finger tips and went onto the balcony to have her breakfast.

Silas's voice returned in her ear, low and steady. "Ivy, as I expected, they're watching you. But listen—act normal. Don't look around. Just follow my voice. This is a good sign. It means they're very interested in you. But you must not give them any reason to be suspicious. Don't try to spot them. Just eat your breakfast. Don't respond—just listen."

Startled, Ivy dropped her spoon onto the floor. Her voice was barely a whisper as she asked, "How do you know these things? Where are you?" Then, quickly recovering, she picked up the spoon, sat back down, and continued her breakfast as if nothing had happened.

"Do not talk to me here," Silas warned, his voice firm but calm. "They may be watching too closely, and even a whisper could raise suspicion. You'll have all your answers later, but today is crucial. So be patient."

His tone shifted slightly, more instructive now. "From now on, whenever you do anything, putting on the fingertip covers as I told you before, cleaning your prints, anything like that, make sure the windows are closed. No movements should be seen from outside."

There was a brief pause before he added, "I'll be with you these next two days. But remember, I can't help you physically. I can only guide you." And just like that, he went silent again.

She needed to kill time. Calmly, she cleaned the table and washed the dishes. Afterward, she sat on the floor and began her yoga poses, focusing on her breath, trying to stay grounded.

Suddenly, Ethan appeared before her. A wave of joy rushed over her—she sprang up and embraced him tightly. "Ethan!" she whispered with relief, then quickly asked, "Do you know anything about Silas?"

But Ethan's expression was serious. "Ivy, right now it's important you focus on your assignment. Don't waste time on anything else. Let's get to that adoption center and find Angela." She nodded, and in an instant, they were there.

They moved silently through the building, searching room by room, but Angela was nowhere to be found. Panic started rising in Ivy's chest. "What happened to her? Where is she?" she cried.

Ethan gently held her shoulders. "Don't worry. We'll find her. Just stay focused. Let's see if there's a hidden room. We're able to see through walls in this form, so let's use that. Come on."

They searched the building from top to bottom, but she was nowhere to be found. Ethan turned to Ivy and asked, "Can you locate her if you focus?" She nodded, closed her eyes, and when she opened them again, there she was. Angela sat alone in a bare room, no furniture except a single bed. She looked frightened, her wide eyes locked on the door. Slowly, she lifted her gaze and looked directly at Ivy, then smiled.

Ivy froze, startled. "Can you see me? Do you hear me?" she asked. But Angela just kept staring, her smile unchanged. She couldn't hear a word.

Ivy scanned the room curiously, then stepped outside. Peering through the walls, she spotted Carl in a room across the hallway. Her heart dropped. She needed to determine exactly where they were. Moving quickly, she slipped outside the building. It was far beyond the city, along a field and an unpaved road. Widening her radius, she swept the surroundings until she saw it.

A rusted sign: **Welcome to Velmoria City**.

The name rang like an echo from a forgotten age. The place was cloaked in ancient mystery, as if its very stones still whispered the wisdom of a lost civilization. Ivy could see the faded marble towers draped in ivy and feel secrets sleeping beneath its crumbled streets.

But even then, she still had no idea where *here* was.

She turned her focus back to Carl. He sat on the floor beside the makeshift bed, his mind in chaos, replaying everything, from the beginning to the moment they murdered his wife. His thoughts clung to one thing: his daughter.

Suddenly, Ivy heightened her frequency, shifting her consciousness to a sharper, more attuned state. Her perception extended like a sonar pulse, sweeping across the terrain. Within seconds, her mind locked onto the coordinates somewhere between Toronto and the edge of the Devil's Glen.

She opened her eyes, a subtle glow behind them and Ethan in front of her when she said, "I found it," her voice calm but charged. "It's located between Toronto and the edge of the Devil's Glen. The place is called Velmoria City. That's where they're keeping Carl and Angela. But what does that have to do with the CIA?

Ethan's eyes narrowed as she continued. "I think they're pressuring Carl to reveal something that he wasn't involved in, something critical they haven't uncovered yet, and they're using Angela to manipulate him. Paul's behind this. That bastard is covering his tracks, and I'm almost certain he plans to eliminate Carl once he gets what he wants."

Ethan glanced at her, concern sharpening his voice. "Not on our watch. That's why we're here. The CIA goes wherever it wants. But right now, you're getting close to your interview, you should head back and start getting ready."

Ivy nodded, then turned to him with a curious edge. "Is Silas watching me all day?"

Ethan met her eyes and explained calmly, "Only for these two days. I asked him to. I trust him with my life. Just keep the earpiece in at all times, and wear the fake fingertips, even inside that apartment. Don't take any chances." She nodded and smiled softly and in the next instant, she was back in the apartment inside her body again.

The moment she began to move, Silas's voice came through the earpiece. "Ivy! I see you've returned. Now, listen carefully and do not respond. As I told you, they're watching, evaluating whether they can trust you. Every move matters now. Stay calm, stay silent, and follow exactly what I say."

"You've got two hours until your interview, and the location is forty-five minutes from where you are. Here's what I need you to do: grab any book, doesn't matter which, and head out to the balcony. Don't search the address. Don't even let your eyes wander. Just sit down in the chair, get comfortable, and read. I want you to stay out there for at least twenty minutes. Stay relaxed, focused. They're watching you, Ivy, because they're planning to hire you. This is part of the test."

She lifted her cellphone and scrolled through the phone, searching—then finally found it. A moment later, a song by Roy Orbison began to play:

"Anything you want, you got it.

Anything you need, you got it.

Anything at all, you got it, baby…"

Silas burst into laughter. "Okay, okay, I got it. Thanks for your answer!" he said between laughs. "Ha ha ha ha!"

Ivy didn't argue anymore. She followed his instructions to the letter. With the book in hand, she sat quietly on the balcony, her posture calm, her mind steady. She didn't just read, she became the character, both the one in the book and the role Silas had prepared her for. She was determined to get this right.

She glanced at the time. It was time to get ready. Downstairs, the cab was already waiting in front of the building.

She arrived at Tina's office ten minutes early for the interview. A receptionist greeted her politely and asked her to wait. Tina was on a call and appeared visibly distracted. Ivy took a seat, calm and composed. She had become experienced at detaching from her body without drawing attention. Ensuring her physical form remained poised and natural, she slipped into spirit form and quietly moved beside Tina.

"I really have no idea what's going on," Tina was saying, her voice low and cautious. "But he seems to be telling the truth. I'll need to investigate further."

Ivy leaned in, wondering who was on the other end of the line, but before she could glean anything more, Tina responded with a firm, "I will," and the line went dead.

Tina stared out the window for a few seconds, caught in a brief moment of daydreaming. Then, snapping back to focus, she pressed a button on her desk and said, "Let Mrs. Tumbleway in."

Ivy returned to her body seamlessly, adjusted her posture, and rose with calm confidence. She stepped into Tina's office and extended her hand with professional grace. "Good afternoon, Mrs. Greenwood. It's a pleasure to finally meet you."

Tina smiled, composed but clearly intrigued, and gestured toward one of the chairs. "Please, have a seat."

As Ivy settled in, Tina studied her for a moment before speaking. "Your home is quite close to here. That's already a plus. Now, according to your resume, you worked at a psychiatric facility as a psychologist for twelve years. We verified the details, they check out. Why did you leave?"

Ivy smiled, though inwardly she was unsettled. Silas hadn't included this detail in the files, and now he was silent. "It became a little too routine for me."

She replied smoothly, "I needed a change."

"That's actually a good point," Tina said, nodding. "I think I might need one myself soon." She leaned forward slightly. "Have you ever had a particularly stubborn patient?"

"Many times," Ivy answered without hesitation. "But I always kept things under control. I know how to calm people down and how to get the answers I need without violence."

Tina sat straighter, her gaze sharpening. She didn't blink. "Tell me how."

Ivy's mind raced. Panic fluttered in her chest. And then, Silas's voice finally came through, steady and reassuring. *"Ivy, you're experienced. You know how to get through to people without hurting them. Trust yourself."*

Her confidence surged back like a wave of strength. "I know how to interact with people, how to read their behavior... even their thoughts. I can tell when someone's lying, or being truthful."

Tina's expression shifted subtly. She stood and walked over to the window, her back now turned to Ivy. "So, you're saying... you can tell what I'm thinking right now?"

Ivy didn't flinch. Sitting perfectly still, her voice remained calm and grounded. "Not like this. I need to hold your hand, close my eyes, and focus, without any interruptions. But yes... I can."

Tina turned and studied her for a few seconds. "Would you be able to show me right now?" A flicker of fear crept into Ivy's chest, though a gentle smile stayed on her lips.

"Go ahead, Ivy. Show her. There's no trick and no magic. You can do this," Silas urged quietly. Ivy nodded, her gaze steady. "Yes, I would."

She stood up and walked toward a love seat tucked into the back of the room. With graceful ease, she sat down and gestured to the spot beside her. Tina moved closer and sat next to her. "May I hold your hand?" Ivy asked.

Tina stretched out her hand without hesitation. Their fingers intertwined.

"Think of something," Ivy whispered. "Anything." She closed her eyes.

This time, she didn't drift entirely out of her body, only her spirit sat upright, face to face with Tina. She stared into her, reaching for a current of thought… but there was nothing. A quiet stillness, as if Tina's mind were a blank slate.

And then he appeared. Ethan stood in front of her. "I'm supposed to read her mind," Ivy said to him silently. "But she's not thinking. I can't see anything. What should I do?"

Ethan studied Tina's face, his expression unreadable. He walked around her slowly, observing every detail, then turned back to Ivy.

"You can't read her mind because she knows how to block you," he said calmly. "She's not thinking in words. She's feeling, observing, processing without language. You can't read what isn't being said, even inside the mind."

He smiled gently at Ivy and said, "I think she's playing with you. Just wait and be patient." But before Ivy could respond, both she and Ethan froze. "Who is this gentleman?" Tina asked through her mind, her voice low and steady. "I can't see him… but I can hear him."

Ivy's breath caught. Her eyes widened in shock. She turned slowly to Ethan, panic rising in her chest. Ethan's expression remained calm, but his eyes locked onto hers. With precise, deliberate gestures, he raised his hands and signed: *Stay calm. Do not panic.*

Ivy's heart pounded, but she forced a steady breath and managed a smile. "It's my conscience talking to me, and it's very helpful," she said softly. Tina narrowed her eyes. "I see."

Without another word, she pulled her hands away and stood up. Ivy instinctively returned to her body and rose to her feet, watching

Tina carefully. Her face was unreadable, no trace of anger, no trace of warmth. Just silence.

Tina stared at her for nearly a minute. To Ivy, it felt like an eternity. Finally, Tina turned, walked back to her desk, and sat down. Her voice, when it came, was cool and precise.

"What is your intention, young lady? What are you doing here? What's your plan? You're playing with fire, and you're not good with fire, because you don't know how to control it. So tell me, why are you here? What's your real interest in entering this institution?"

Silas's voice cut in, urgent and clear. "Ivy! Ethan said she's playing with you. She didn't hear anything, which was her trick. And you, unconsciously, played right into it. She hasn't heard Ethan at all. He's here, and he's the one who heard her mind. She thinks you're innocent... harmless. That's what she truly believes. "Ivy, listen carefully," Ethan says, his voice low and urgent. "Stand up and try to leave, but do it slowly."

Ivy blinked, her mind racing to catch up. Tina's expression, her sudden withdrawal, it was all a performance. A test.

Ivy was scared to death, and hearing Silas's words only tightened the knot in her chest. It was enough. Her hands trembled slightly as she gathered her belongings and stood up.

She looked Tina directly in the eyes, her voice steady but edged with hurt. "I really have no idea why I'm here. But what's become very clear is that there's no respect for individuals in this place. I've had enough of this nonsense."

She took a step back, her gaze unwavering. "I think you should look for someone who matches your quality. Because clearly, I'm not it."

As she turned to leave, Tina suddenly stood up as well and raised a hand, gesturing firmly toward the chair. "Please, Mrs. Tumbleway. May I call you Beatrice?" Ivy hesitated, eyes narrowing slightly, then gave a small nod. "Yes, please." She sat back down, cautiously.

Tina's expression softened just enough to be noticeable. "You know, Beatrice… you are exactly our type. You did precisely what was right. If you had said nothing, just sat there quietly, hoping to be accepted, I wouldn't have wanted you."

She paused, letting the silence sharpen the moment, her eyes never leaving Ivy's. Then she asked, with calm precision, "Would you be able to start tomorrow morning?" Ivy stared at her, trying to determine if this was another test, another game to measure her reactions.

"I assure you, this is not a test," Tina said smoothly, as if reading her thoughts. "It's a genuine offer." Ivy wasn't sure whether Tina had read her mind or simply made a very good guess. Either way, Tina's gaze remained locked on hers, unwavering. "You look confused," she added.

Ivy slowly stood, steadying her voice. "Should I come here… or where exactly should I report tomorrow morning?"

Tina's tone was clear, crisp, and formal. "Tomorrow morning, you are to report here, to my office." Ivy gave a single nod. Without another word, she turned and walked out, the door clicking softly shut behind her.

Ivy was stunned by the news of her hiring and puzzled by the reason behind it. Still, one thing was clear: she had to get closer to Angela, see her with her own eyes, and find a way to get her out, to somewhere safe, somewhere far from all of this.

As soon as she stepped out of the building, Silas's voice filtered through. "Ivy, congratulations, you got the job. Now we can begin our plan. But not face-to-face. We'll keep our communication like this, from a distance. They're watching you closely. You're new, and they don't trust you."

Ivy opened her mouth to respond, but Silas continued without pause. "And one more thing, when you speak to me, make sure your mouth is obscured or turned away. Like I said, they're watching you. Always."

"Are you coming to pick me up, or should I call a cab?" Ivy asked, carefully angling her face so her mouth wasn't visible.

"You can't use your phone to call me," Silas replied calmly. "Now that you're hired, they're monitoring your calls, listening, tracking, watching. They'll trace every number you dial to see if you're playing by their rules. So take a cab or ride the bus. But if you ever need help, talk to me this way. If I'm not around, Ethan will step in. We're with you, Ivy, every step you take."

Ivy smiled and headed toward the bus stop. Without hesitation, she returned to the temporary apartment and quietly began to plan her next move. *I need to slip out again,* she thought, *to speak with Ethan… and to find Angela and Carl.*

Each time she slipped, she moved faster, more effortlessly. She always made sure her body appeared to be napping, just in case. The moment she detached, Ethan was there, waiting.

"You were amazing, Ivy," he said with a proud smile. "I'm so proud of you. Now, let's go find Angela."

"No, first, let's check on Alina and Emma. And I want to make sure Liam's alright," Ivy said.

In an instant, they were beside Liam, who was deep in conversation with his partner in the office. Despite his composed appearance, his thoughts betrayed him. *Where are you, Ivy? I miss you.* Ivy's heart sank. She missed him, too.

They moved on to Emma, who was busy at work. Just then, Alina appeared before them, eyes wide with concern. "Ivy! Where have you been? We were so worried about you. Ethan told me what you're trying to do. I want to help, if I may."

Ivy's face lit up. "Thank you, Alina. I'll let you know. But there's something you can do for me now. Please contact my boyfriend, Liam. Tell him I'm okay, and that I'm working on something important. I can't reach out for security reasons, but I will the moment it's safe."

"Of course," Alina replied without hesitation. Ivy repeated Liam's number twice to make sure it was right. Then, all together, they headed to Velmoria to figure out how to enter without being seen.

They appeared beside Angela, who sat quietly in a room with a handful of other children. "At least she's not alone," Ivy whispered, a wave of relief softening her chest.

They circled the perimeter of the building. Every entrance was locked with a keypad. "You need a pass-code or a card to get in," Ethan noted.

Ivy nodded just as a man approached one of the doors. He scanned his access card and stepped inside. Without a word, Ivy, Ethan, and Alina slipped in behind him.

He made his way to a security room lined with monitors and surveillance feeds. Two other guards were inside, scanning the screens. Ivy froze. The sight overwhelmed her, this wasn't going to be easy. She looked at Ethan, her face etched with doubt.

Ethan met her gaze and gently said, "Don't worry. We'll figure it out." He glanced around, thinking quickly. "Let me go find Silas. He knows these systems better than I do. While I'm gone, I'll keep watch over your place, make sure everything's still safe." Ivy smiled faintly and nodded, trusting him without needing to say a word.

Ivy turned to Silas, a gleam in her eye. "God, I love this realm. Fast and effortless transportation." She flashed him a smile.

Silas chuckled and returned the smile. "Let me take a look at their security system. Seems a little different than before. I think they've upgraded it." With that, he disappeared into the building.

Left behind, Ivy glanced at Alina. "There are four entrances, all heavily secured. Let's see if there's a window… or maybe a hidden door without surveillance." Alina gave a firm nod. "Let's do it."

Silas returned, his face lit with excitement. He looked at Ivy and said, "I might be able to create a pass card for you. I gathered everything I needed from one of the employees, who only shows up once or twice a week."

Ivy's face brightened with hope. "And if that doesn't work, they'll give me a pass card eventually anyway. I'll just use mine. It's not under my real name, and honestly, who cares if they find out I took her?"

Silas's expression shifted immediately, his joy fading into concern. "No, Ivy. That's far too dangerous. The goal is to keep all attention away from you and from your false identity. If they realize why you really came here, they won't stop. They'll scan every face in this country until they find you."

Alina glanced at the clock on the wall and said, "Anyway, I have to go. My class is ending, I'll call Liam." Ivy gave her a grateful smile. "Thanks, Alina."

Then she turned to Silas, her tone shifting. "I want to go to Marcus. I need to know what really happened with the package." Silas nodded, and in the next moment, they were beside Marcus.

He sat rigid in what resembled an interrogation room, silently bracing against Paul's fury. Paul paced like a predator, his voice slicing through the air. "Are you sure?" Marcus swallowed hard, his voice unsteady. "Yes… I'm sure about that."

Paul's eyes blazed with cold rage. "You'd better keep that to yourself. If they find out you took the package on my orders, you'll be dead before they even touch you because I won't let you, or anyone else, drag me down. I'm watching you."

He stormed out, the door slamming behind him. Marcus sat trembling, his hands shaking as he gave a barely perceptible nod, fear written across his face.

"Ivy, you were right, Carl is innocent," Silas said quietly. "We have to do something… but these people hold real power, and they're dangerous. Don't forget that." Ivy nodded, her face solemn. She understood.

They turned their attention back to Marcus, trying to read his thoughts—but there was nothing. His mind was a blank wall of fear. Maybe he was too terrified to even think. So they waited, silent, still, until his breathing slowed and the tremble in his hands began to fade.

God… my family's in danger. I don't know what to do. Marcus's thoughts finally surfaced, heavy and panicked. *Either way, they're going to kill me. Once this is over, Paul won't risk anyone knowing about the packages, he'll do anything to keep himself safe.*

His inner voice wavered. *Maybe if I end it myself… maybe then he'll leave my family alone.*

Ivy looked at Silas, her eyes filled with concern. "He's in danger, too. Paul is the chief of police in this area. Of course, his word carries more weight in public than a driver's."

Silas nodded. "You're right. But remember, Paul is only the chief in this region, not the entire state." Ivy frowned, confused. "What do you mean? Who's above him?"

Silas met her gaze with quiet confidence. "His name is Chief Darius Holt. He's the state chief of police and very popular among the people."

Ivy's expression shifted, a hopeful smile brightening her face. It made her look even more radiant. "Maybe we should go to him, tell him everything?"

Silas gently shook his head, a shadow passing over his eyes. "No, Ivy. We don't have a single piece of solid evidence. How would you even explain what you saw? Were you a witness? How? Paul's too smart, he'll twist it all around and pin everything on you. Without proof, you can't touch him."

"Silas, can I still drive the car I've been using since the first day I went to that apartment?" Ivy asked, her uneasiness showing clearly in her eyes.

"No," Silas replied calmly. "That car was rented under your false identity, just to support your cover. You need to return it as soon as possible, or they'll be additional charges."

Ivy frowned. "But wouldn't those charges go to the fake credit card? So… what's the problem?"

Silas noticed the tension in her posture, the discomfort of being without transportation. "Yes," he said gently, "but once the funds on that card run dry, the company will start asking questions. And the more questions they ask, the more suspicious everything becomes."

Ethan appeared beside them, his voice light but direct. "Hey guys, I can't stay long, but I wanted to let you know. It's okay to keep the car as long as you're undercover. We'll handle the credit card."

Silas turned to Ivy with a small smile, shrugging. "Well... looks like your problem's been solved."

After a brief pause, his tone grew more grounded. "Go back to the apartment and get some rest. You need to be ready for your first day tomorrow morning. We'll figure out our next move soon. Don't worry, we're not leaving them to face this alone."

Ivy smiled, gave him a quick, grateful hug, and in the next instant, she was back in the apartment. Her eyes fluttered open. She sat up slowly, then turned to gaze out over the balcony, the city lights flickering like quiet thoughts on the edge of night.

The next morning, she arrived at Tina's office ten minutes early. Fear twisted quietly inside her, uncertainty, nerves, and a subtle dread of Tina's unreadable stare. Her presence was always unsettling. Her eyes didn't seem to blink.

Suddenly, the office door swung open, and Tina appeared in the doorway like a statue come to life. She looked directly at Ivy. "Please come in, Beatrice."

Without another word, she turned and walked back inside. Ivy stood up immediately and stepped in after her, finding Tina already seated behind her desk. "Good morning, Mrs. Greenwood," Ivy said politely. Tina didn't look up. "Please. Have a seat."

Ivy sat in silence for a while, the room thick with tension. Tina methodically flipped through pages, one after another, without looking up. Finally, she stopped, raised her eyes, and locked them onto Ivy.

"I hope you completed your assignment and familiarized yourself with our policies," she said flatly. Without waiting for a response, she pressed on.

"It is absolutely essential to follow the rules and regulations here. You'll be working in the daycare area, as you know. But let me be clear, I don't want any of the children becoming emotionally attached to you. They must learn to follow you, not cling to you. There are no cozy corners here."

Her tone shifted slightly, just enough to feel intentional. "At the same time, I want the children to appear comfortable when you're present. When prospective parents visit, I expect you to bring the child to them and behave in a way that assures the couple that we provide a safe, structured environment. Do you understand your role here?"

Her gaze was piercing, unblinking. Ivy held her composure and answered with calm precision, "Yes, Mrs. Greenwood. I understand."

Tina continued to stare at her without so much as a twitch. "Call me Tina. It shows how friendly we are here, especially in front of clients."

Ivy gave a subtle nod. "I will. Thanks, Tina."

Tina's eyes remained fixed on Ivy for another beat, as if scanning beneath her calm exterior. Then, without a word, she stood and walked over to a nearby cabinet, retrieving a small folder and a staff badge. She returned and placed them on the desk between them.

"This contains your access codes and a basic schedule," she said, her voice clipped and mechanical. "You'll be supervised for the first few days. We rotate staff often, so don't get too familiar with anyone."

She leaned back in her chair, fingers steepled with precision. "If you see anything unusual, anything at all, you report it. Immediately. Not later. Not tomorrow. And never assume it's not your business."

The room fell into a tense, deliberate silence. "Your badge is authorized only during your scheduled hours. Come on time, leave on time. Otherwise, you'll be creating problems for yourself."

Without another word, Tina stood and walked into the hallway. Ivy rose quickly and followed her, her heart already tightening in her chest.

They passed one hallway after another, a maze of doors and muted colors, until they reached a room Ivy immediately recognized. It was the same room she had visited yesterday with Silas and Alina.

Her eyes darted to the spot where Angela had been seated, but it was empty. In fact, Angela wasn't in the room at all. Panic crept up her spine. She scanned the faces of the other children, but Angela was nowhere to be found.

Before she could ask, Tina turned to her, expression unreadable. "Beatrice, this is Rosie. She'll train you for a few days. After that, you're on your own."

Ivy gave Rosie a polite nod. "Hi." Then, trying to sound casual, she asked, "Are these all the children I'll be responsible for, or are there more?"

Rosie smiled kindly. "A few are in the clinic. They weren't feeling well." Tension gripped Ivy's shoulders. She forced herself to nod. Tina gave her one last unreadable look, then turned and left the room without another word.

Rosie appeared calm and polite, her voice gentle as she walked Ivy through the daily routine. She pointed out the rooms designated for meals, naps, and playtime, moving with a practiced ease.

"What are the names of the children?" Ivy asked, scanning the room.

Rosie gestured toward the small chairs and neatly made beds. "Their names are marked on their chairs and beds. That helps us keep everything organized."

Ivy looked around, taking in the names one by one, then asked softly, "Would it be all alright if I familiarized myself with their names?"

Rosie gave a warm smile. "Not at all, it's actually a great first step in getting to know them."

Ivy began moving quietly through the room, reading each name with care. When she finally spotted Angela's name, something in her chest eased. *At least she's still listed here,* she thought. A small flicker of hope returned.

"What's wrong with the children in the clinic? What kind of illness do they have?" Ivy asked, her voice steady but edged with concern. A quiet fear tugged at her, what if they were hurting Angela to get answers from Carl?

Rosie remained calm as she replied, "There's a cold going around. That's all. It spreads quickly between the little ones, so we have to be extra cautious. As soon as we notice symptoms, we separate them from the healthy group to prevent further spread." Ivy nodded, but the unease in her chest didn't fully lift.

"When will they be picked up from the clinic?" Ivy asked, her voice full of eagerness to finally see Angela in person. Rosie glanced at her from the side and replied calmly, "They'll stay there until the doctor says it's safe."

"Have you dealt with a similar situation before? And how long does it usually take for the doctor to authorize their release?" Ivy asked. Despite the risk, she spoke with the calm assurance of someone seasoned.

Rosie continued stacking blocks with one of the little boys, silent for a moment. Finally, she spoke without looking up, "Look,

Beatrice, just focus on your job and do what you're supposed to. When they're ready to come back, I'll let you know." She raised her eyebrows and shoulders in a half-shrug, then turned back to the child, resuming the game as if the conversation had never happened.

Ivy was exhausted, drained by the endless tasks expected of her, and the truth was, she was never good with children. But she had no choice. She had to endure it all, for as long as it took, until the moment came when she could take Angela and get her out of this place.

Rosie approached quietly, waiting for Ivy to finish feeding one of the children. As soon as she was done, Rosie offered a polite smile. "You can take your break now. It's a one-hour lunch. Be back exactly at one." Without waiting for a reply, she turned and walked over to the lunch table where the children were finishing their meals and preparing for their daily nap.

Ivy stood up, glanced around the room, then looked over at Rosie. Without a word, she walked to her locker, grabbed her things, and made her way to the cafeteria on the far side of the building. Only a few people were scattered around, quietly eating. She chose a table in the corner, sat down, and ordered her lunch. As she waited, she adjusted her posture carefully, making sure she was steady enough not to fall over during her float out.

Ethan stood in front of her, smiling, and just seeing him made her   feel   lighter. "I shouldn't go far," she said, glancing toward the counter. "My lunch will be ready any minute. But I'm worried about Angela. Is she okay? Where exactly is she?"

Ethan's expression softened as he listened. Then, calmly, he said, "Don't worry about Angela. She's in the clinic, just like they told you. But be careful with Rosie, she's not just a caregiver. She's head of security here, and she's watching you."

Ivy's eyes widened in surprise. She nodded slowly, absorbing every word. Ethan smiled and added, "Here's your lunch. And remember, it's your first day. We'll make a plan to get Angela. See you soon." She nodded again, and in an instant, her soul slipped back into place, reuniting with her body.

Ethan stood quietly in the room with Angela and another child. Angela sat with her head down, her small face heavy with sadness. She was too young to understand, too young to grasp that her mother was gone for good. The ache of not seeing her parents gnawed at her, and all Ethan could feel from her was quiet despair.

He looked around and spotted Carl, slumped on a narrow bed, pale and hollow-eyed. The man looked like a shadow of himself, grieving the loss of his wife and terrified for his daughter's fate.

Carl's mind was spinning. He kept going back to the day of the delivery. Paul had placed the order. Carl, along with Marcus and Billy, had handled the transport. Marcus was behind the wheel. Carl had signed the receipt when the packages were loaded into the car. Billy left right after.

Everything had gone according to plan until it didn't. They reached Paul's building, parked in the designated spot, and were instructed to leave the car. There was a short window between when Carl left to hand in the paperwork and when Paul arrived. When Carl returned, the boxes were untouched, exactly where they'd been left.

But when Paul opened them, they were empty. How? How could that be? Had Marcus switched them out? Was he working with Paul, or was he just as deep in the mess as Carl now found himself? Either way, something wasn't right. And Carl knew the clock was ticking.

Ethan saw Paul approaching Carl's cell in the hallway, his steps calm, his smile calculated. The security guard unlocked the door, and Paul slipped inside with a hint of smugness on his face.

Ethan focused, tuning into Paul's thoughts as they surfaced, sharp and sinister, *"If I can convince him to take the blame, then I'll have the perfect excuse to send him to the mystery land of no return."*

Carl stood up at once, his weary face lifted toward Paul, searching for a trace of understanding, some sign that his innocence mattered. But Paul wasn't there for the truth. He already knew it. He paced slowly, deliberately, back and forth across the narrow room, then halted in front of Carl without a word, his eyes fixed and unblinking.

"Paul! I've been honest with you from the beginning, I still am. I have no idea what happened to the packages. Marcus was there too. I had to leave for a moment to get the paperwork signed, and when I came back, Marcus was already in the truck. I got in and we drove off. If anything was missing, it must've happened before—when the packages were first brought in."

Carl's face had drained of color. The weight of accusation, of not knowing who to trust, clung to him like a sickness.

"Did you check them, one-by-one, to make sure they were pure?" Paul's expression darkened, his tone sharpening like a blade.

Carl nodded quickly. "I checked one package from each box. They were there—pure, and the best quality."

Without warning, Paul shoved him hard. Carl stumbled backward and collapsed onto the edge of the bed. He caught himself, breath shallow, and pushed up immediately, standing again with trembling resolve.

Carl stared at him, confused and searching. "Shouldn't you ask Marcus what happened while I was gone to get the papers? He was there, he must know something."

Paul's face twisted with anger, and he barked, "Marcus was just the driver! It was your responsibility to ensure a safe delivery!"

Carl held his gaze, unshaken now, his voice steady. "It looks to me like you're trying to pin this on me… no matter what the truth is." Paul's fury erupted. He struck Carl with such force that his body flew sideways, slamming into the wall with a sickening thud.

Carl sat slumped against the wall, motionless, the sting of the blow still echoing through his body. In a daze, he turned his head toward Paul, his voice low and cracked. "If you've already decided to do something to me, go ahead. It's clear you've made up your mind to accuse me. But please… don't hurt my little girl. She's just a child."

Paul paused, his eyes narrowing with chilling precision. He stepped over to the table beside the bed and placed a notebook and a pen down with quiet finality. "Then write it. Sign that you're responsible for the damage, and your little girl will be placed with a good family."

He didn't wait for an answer. He turned and walked out, the door whispering shut behind him like a verdict.

Ethan couldn't believe what he had just witnessed. A sick heaviness settled in his chest as he watched Carl, broken and cornered. The injustice clawed at him. He stood there for a moment, torn between rage and helplessness, then turned and slipped out the way he had come, silent, unseen, but burning inside.

CHAPTER SIX – Whispers of a Plan Beneath the Dream

Ivy, worn to the bone, sank into the lounge chair on the balcony. The air was cool and gentle, wrapping around her like a lullaby. Within moments, sleep claimed her.

Her body stayed behind, but she did not. Her spirit, light and unburdened, stepped free. And Ethan was already there, waiting his presence glowing faintly, steady as always. She turned to him, her voice echoing in that quiet, boundless space. "Working there is so hard… my body's exhausted."

Ethan didn't reply right away. He simply watched her with a calm that felt older than time itself. Ivy tilted her head, searching his eyes. "What's going on with you?" she asked, her voice clear now, spirit to spirit, where no mask could remain.

Ethan looked at her, his face heavy with the weight of what he'd seen. "You were right, Ivy. We should've acted sooner. What Paul did to Carl… it's unforgivable. We have to help him."

Ivy's heart sank. She nodded, her voice firm despite the ache in her chest. "Then we start planning. Is Silas able to make a pass card? If so, we can go at night, get them both out. By tomorrow, I'll be gone anyway."

Ethan stepped closer, his hands resting gently on her shoulders, grounding her in the moment. "We'll go to Carl's tonight. When he's asleep, we'll speak to him, spirit to spirit, explain everything. Meanwhile, we'll scan the area and count the guards. We need to know exactly what we're walking into."

A spark lit in Ivy's eyes. She smiled, the first real one in days, and nodded with a quiet fire. "Let's go."

Carl sat on the cold floor, his back against the wall, his spirit hollow, like a man who had surrendered not only his freedom but his final thread of hope. The notebook lay open beside him, its pages filled with shaky handwriting. In it, he had falsely confessed, taking full responsibility for the missing packages.

Ethan knelt beside the notebook, scanning the words with a growing fury. Then he turned to Ivy, his voice tight with disbelief. "It's not right. He didn't do anything. He followed Paul's orders, every step. And he doesn't realize the danger he's in now. Paul's not going to let this end here. He's planning to hand him over to Dante Morado… and they won't just kill him."

He paused, his voice dropping into something darker. "They'll make him disappear, painfully."

As soon as Ethan finished speaking, Ivy reached out and pointed silently toward Carl. Ethan turned, and there it was. Carl's spirit, rising just above his body, confused and flickering like a flame caught in the wind. He looked around, disoriented, until his eyes met theirs.

"Who are you? Where am I?" he asked, his voice echoing slightly in the stillness of that space between the physical and the unseen. Ethan stepped forward with a calm, reassuring smile. "We're your guardian angels, Carl. We're here because we're worried about you and about Angela. And we're here to help."

Carl stared at them, the confusion on his face slowly giving way to something else, something brighter. A faint glow of hope began to shimmer around him, growing with every word. "How can you help me?" he asked, his voice trembling.

Ethan spoke gently but firmly. "We need your cooperation. We're going to get you and your daughter out of here. But listen closely, do not trust anyone in this place. The only people you can rely on are the ones who give you a specific code: 8877. Remember that. That number is your signal."

Ivy stepped forward, her voice steady with conviction. "I saw everything. I saw how Paul murdered your wife, took your daughter, and locked you away like a criminal. We won't rest until both of you are free."

Carl's expression cracked into a fragile smile. "Okay… When?"

Ethan laid a comforting hand on his shoulder, anchoring him. "Tomorrow night. No hesitation, no questions, just follow the person who gives you the code. They're the one who'll lead you out."

Carl nodded slowly, absorbing every word. "Okay. Do you… do you know where Angela is now?" Ivy met his gaze, her voice soft but resolute. "Yes, I do. Come with us. Let's go see your daughter."

In an instant, they were there, hovering gently above Angela's bed. She lay asleep, peaceful and radiant, her small hands tucked under her cheek. The soft rise and fall of her breath was like a lullaby echoing through the stillness.

Carl's eyes filled with emotion as he looked down at her. For the first time in so long, he felt something real joy. Pure, aching joy. Ivy smiled at him and gently pointed to the foot of the bed.

Carl turned, and there she was. Angela's spirit had risen too, glowing with a soft, golden light, as if the universe itself had wrapped her in love. She looked up and saw him, her eyes widening with wonder. "Daddy!" she cried, running to him.

Carl fell to his knees and caught her in his arms, holding her as if he'd never let go again. "Oh, sweetheart…"

Angela looked up at him with the trusting eyes only a child could have. "Daddy, when are you coming to pick me up?" Carl smiled through the tears rising in his throat. "Very soon, my angel. I'm coming for you… very soon."

Carl woke in his cell, the cold reality swallowing him whole. He looked around, eyes adjusting to the dimness, and a heavy sigh escaped his chest. "It was only a dream," he whispered to himself, the words tasting like ash.

He leaned back against the wall, and without resistance, the tears came—trickling down his eyes, his cheeks, soaking silently into his face. His gaze drifted across the room, hollow and hopeless. In the unseen space beside him, Ethan turned to Ivy, his tone focused. "We have to begin the plan for tomorrow night. I'll go to Silas. He can create a pass card."

He paused, then added, "I checked the schedule. Tomorrow night, Mathew Bubba is on duty as a security guard, and Elise Talia is the babysitter assigned. I'll confirm everything and let you know." Ivy nodded, her eyes steady. The rescue had already begun.

The next morning, Ivy arrived exactly on time, her steps calm but her heart racing beneath the surface. Rosie greeted her with a warm smile and pointed toward the glass window of the clinic.

Ivy followed her gesture, and there they were. Angela, along with the other child, sitting quietly inside. Their cheeks no longer pale, their little hands busy with toys.

"They're alright," Rosie said gently. "The doctor cleared them this morning. They can join the other children now."

Ivy smiled, doing her best to contain the surge of joy rising in her chest. She didn't want to draw attention. But inside, she was glowing. She gave a small nod, her voice steady. "That's good to hear."

Ivy joined one of the tables where the children were drawing, blending in naturally, her eyes occasionally drifting to Angela. After a moment, she turned casually to Rosie and asked, "I think I prefer night shifts. It's quiet… easier in some ways. Do you think I could be considered for the night schedule?"

Rosie smiled gently but shook her head. "Not now. You're not trained for that."

Ivy was caught off guard. Her brow furrowed as she looked back at her. "Why would I need training to be here at night, when the children are asleep?"

Rosie gave a small, knowing sigh and tilted her head. "I know it sounds confusing… but you don't understand what the night shift involves. This place is part of a protected agency. These children… most of them belong to high-risk individuals. Some are criminals. We've had break-ins before, and they've become more frequent."

She leaned in slightly, her tone lowering. "That's why anyone working nights must be trained in how to defend the children and themselves."

Ivy's heart sank. Tonight was going to be far more dangerous than she'd anticipated. Her mind raced through possibilities, but her thoughts were abruptly interrupted by the sound of a child crying.

She turned sharply and saw Angela on the floor, her small face crumpled in pain. Rosie began walking toward her, but Ivy was already moving faster.

She reached Angela first and dropped to her knees, wrapping the little girl in a protective embrace. Holding her close, Ivy looked back at Rosie and said softly but firmly, "Don't worry, I've got her."

She rocked Angela gently in her arms, her voice low and soothing. "Don't worry, sweetheart… everything's going to be alright. I promise." Ivy looked at Rosie, curiosity and concern mingling in her eyes. "Were you trained for the night shift?"

Rosie let out a dry chuckle and glanced at her sideways. "Yes… and you have no idea how hard it was."

She paused, her smile turning rueful. "Six months of training. Every single day. Two broken ribs, three fractures, and more times than I can count, my shoulder had to be popped back into place by the doctors." She shook her head lightly. "You don't want to know."

"Are you still doing night shifts, or have you given up?" Ivy asked, her tone casual but her eyes watchful. Rosie lifted her chin slightly, her confidence returning. "Of course, I still do night shifts. I was trained for them, remember?"

Ivy leaned in a little. "Have you ever caught an intruder?" Rosie's face lit with a touch of pride. "Of course I have. I'm a nightmare to intruders," she said with a wink.

Ivy smiled faintly. "That's good to know. I might be interested." Rosie returned the smile and exited the room, her footsteps fading down the hallway.

Left alone, Ivy's expression changed. A knot of unease tightened in her chest. Was Rosie telling the truth? Or was she exaggerating, maybe trying to intimidate her, or simply testing how much Ivy could handle? Either way, it was clear: they didn't trust her yet... and tonight, she would have to walk a very dangerous line.

Time was up, and she quietly prepared to go home. In no time, she was back in her apartment. She made herself dinner and ate it on the balcony, letting the evening air calm her nerves. This was her way of centering herself. She needed to ensure her body was relaxed, that nothing would jolt her awake in the middle of what was coming. She changed, settled into bed, and adjusted her body into the most restful position possible. In no time, her spirit floated out, then Silas appeared. Looks like he was already there and waiting for her.

She felt a quiet wave of relief at the sight of him, though a flicker of nervousness lingered. "Are you here all the time? Even when I changed into my night clothes?"

Silas shifted slightly, a faint, awkward smile tugging at his lips. "I'm not allowed to watch you when you're changing, showering, or during your private time. That's Ethan's order."

Ivy relaxed a little, her voice more assured now. "Good. So… are we doing it tonight?"

Silas gave a small nod. "Yes."

He looked straight into her eyes, his voice low and firm. "Are you ready or not? Because this is a very dangerous mission."

"Yes, I am. Tell me what you did," she replied, her voice steady.

Silas explained, "We hacked their cameras—Ethan is watching us and guiding everything. We created a pass card. In forty-five minutes, you should be ready to leave. You won't be coming back here. Use the back exit of this building and head to the next street over. Don't go out the front. I'll meet you on the back street. I'll give you an earpiece that connects us with Ethan. He has full access to the maps and cameras inside Haven Reach Institute. He'll guide us step by step."

Silas's tone became firmer. "Once inside, you find Angela. I'll find Carl. We'll stay connected the entire time through the earpieces. I'll take Carl and Angela to a safe house. You go straight home. And don't forget your fingertip covers."

He paused, then added gravely, "They're planning to get rid of him by tomorrow. That's why we have to move tonight." Ivy's expression darkened with fear. But Silas smiled gently. "Don't worry. We'll save them." She nodded and smiled faintly. "Sure. See you in forty-five minutes." Silas left

Ivy returned to her body, but couldn't wake up. Panic whispered at the edges of her mind. *What's going on?* she wondered. *Why can't I move?*

"Ah, too much relaxation is not good," she muttered in her spirit form, trying again, harder this time. Nothing. Her body remained still, stubbornly unresponsive. A flicker of worry tightened in her chest.

She tried to reach Silas. Nothing. Ethan, still nothing. They were both in physical form now, completely out of reach.

Desperate, she flew to Alina, who was in the middle of a classroom session, calmly instructing a group of new students. Ivy hovered in the doorway, trying to catch her attention, but the panic inside her was rising fast.

This is not right.

Suddenly, a powerful force pulled her downward—no warning, no resistance. She was yanked violently into her body. She shot upright in bed just as her phone blared to life beside her. Heart racing, she snatched it up.

"Thank God," she gasped, breathless. "If the phone hadn't rung, I was screwed." She pressed the phone to her ear. "Hello?" A cold voice came through the line: "You're late." Then the line went dead.

She threw on her clothes and bolted out the back of the building. The street was empty—unnervingly quiet, cloaked in shadows. Her eyes scanned the darkness, searching for Silas. But he was nowhere in sight. A flicker of panic rose in her chest.

Suddenly, a voice pierced the stillness from behind. "Why were you late?"

She jolted and spun around. Silas stood there, his eyes sharp. "I... I don't know," she stammered. "I couldn't get back into my body. I think I was too relaxed... but thank you for calling me and waking me up."

Silas's expression didn't change. "I didn't call you." Ivy froze. Her face drained of color. "Then... who was it?" A faint smile crossed his lips. "Ethan."

Before she could respond, he took her hand. "It doesn't matter now. We have to go." They ran down the street toward two parked bikes. Ivy hesitated. "What is this? Do you want us to bike there?" Silas grinned. "Do you have a better idea?" She sighed. "No."

He handed her a small earpiece. "Put this on. You'll be able to hear Ethan—he'll be with us the whole night. Don't speak, just listen. If you need to respond, tap the earpiece once for yes, twice for no." Ivy nodded and placed it in her ear. The night had officially begun.

They reached a spot just far enough from the daycare building, concealed in the deep shadows stretching across the quiet street. The building loomed ahead, silent, dimly lit, and ominous. Ivy turned to Silas, her voice low. "What now?"

Silas gave her a pointed look, the corners of his mouth curling into a half-smile. "It's not a party. We wait for Ethan. I told you, don't talk, only listen. From this moment on, we move when Ethan says move."

Ivy nodded again, her expression serious now, the weight of the moment settling in her chest. She fixed her eyes on the building, heart steadying, waiting for the voice in her ear to guide them into the unknown.

"Security is out of the room to check around. Go now," Ethan's voice came crisply through the earpiece. Without hesitation, they sprinted across the street, keeping low, their footsteps silent against the pavement. The back door of the building loomed ahead.

Ivy slowed just enough to glance up at the camera above the door. She pointed to it urgently, her eyes darting to Silas. He followed her gaze, then met her eyes calmly.

They heard Ethan's voice through the earpiece, "Don't worry about that," he said, his voice steady. "I'm the only one seeing you now. The real footage is already being wiped. Nothing will be left." Ivy nodded, tension still thrumming through her, but she trusted him. They turned to the door. It was time.

A soft click echoed from the lock, barely audible, but enough. The door creaked open on its own. They both stared at it for a second, then glanced at each other. Neither of them had touched it.

Ethan's voice came through again, calm and precise. "Go now. After you enter, turn right in the hallway." Without a word, they slipped inside, their movements swift and silent, vanishing into the dim corridor as the door whispered shut behind them.

At the end of the hallway, they paused in the silence, the dim lights casting long shadows on the floor. Silas paused for a brief moment and looked up at the small camera tucked into the corner of the ceiling. Its red light blinked steadily, watching, but not recording, not anymore.

Ethan's voice came through, crisp and steady in their ears. "Ivy, go right. At the end of the hallway on your right is the children's bedroom. Find Angela and return to the door you just entered. Get out with her, then cross the street to where your bikes are. Wait in the shadows until Silas joins you."

Ivy gave a silent nod and slipped into the corridor, her footsteps no louder than a whisper of breath.

"Silas," Ethan continued, "go left. At the first hallway, turn left again. You'll see a staircase. Take it down. There'll be a door at the bottom. Wait there until I tell you it's safe to move." Silas gave a firm nod, then looked up at the nearest camera and raised a thumbs-up.

"He's on the second floor. You're safe. Go," Ethan's voice instructed calmly. Silas gave a subtle nod, his expression unwavering, then descended into the stairwell's shadowed silence.

"There's a narrow door ahead, open it and get into that hallway," Ethan continued. "Go to the third door. Carl will be inside. You'll have to unlock it manually. I can't do it from here."

Silas moved with quiet urgency. He reached the narrow door, eased it open, and slipped into the hallway. Counting doors quickly—one… two… three—he knelt before the third. From his coat, he pulled out a compact set of tools and went to work on the lock. His hands moved with practiced speed.

Two minutes later, the lock clicked softly. He opened the door slowly, just a crack—and immediately locked eyes with Carl, who was standing beside the bed, eyes wide, face pale. His hands trembled at his sides.

"Please… don't hurt my little girl," Carl whispered, his voice shaking. "If you want to kill me, go ahead… just leave my daughter alone."

Silas stepped fully into the room, his voice calm and quiet. "Code 7788. Do you remember that? I'm not here to hurt anyone. I'm here to take you both to safety."

Carl's brows drew together in confusion, his breath shallow. He didn't move. Silas took a slow step closer. "7788," he said again, gently. "I gave you that code in your dream. You remember, don't you? I'm not your enemy. I'm here to get you and your daughter out tonight."

Carl blinked again, the tension in his face slowly beginning to melt. His shoulders dropped slightly, and he gave a quick, repeated nod.

"How did you manage to come into my dream?" he whispered, eyes wide with awe. "I thought it was just a dream… Oh my God, thank you…"

Silas reached out and shook his hand firmly, then raised a finger to his lips in a silent signal. *No talking. Just follow.* "We don't have time for explanations right now," he said softly.

Carl nodded again, understanding. He stepped in behind Silas, quiet as a shadow, and together they slipped back into the hallway, one step closer to freedom.

On the other side of the building, Ivy quietly slipped into the children's room, the soft hush of breathing filling the dimly lit space. She moved gently between the small beds, her eyes scanning the sleeping faces until she found her, Angela.

She knelt beside her and brushed a hand through the girl's soft hair. Angela stirred, her eyes fluttering open. "Would you hug me?" she whispered.

Ivy wrapped her arms around her without hesitation and gently lifted her. "Do you want to go with me?" she asked softly. Angela nodded, a sleepy smile forming. "But you have to promise me not to talk until I tell you to, okay?" Angela nodded again, silently.

Ivy cradled her close and turned toward the door, only to hear Ethan's voice in her earpiece, tense and urgent: **"Ivy! Elise is heading toward the children's bedroom. Put Angela back in her bed and hide, now."**

Panic prickled at Ivy's skin. Her heartbeat quickened. She looked into Angela's eyes and whispered quickly, "If you want to see your dad, you have to pretend you're sleeping. When Elise leaves, I'll take you to him. It's our secret, okay?"

Angela nodded again, her little face serious. Ivy gently laid her back down, tucking her in as if nothing had happened. Then, with no time to waste, she scanned the room, her eyes landed on a small closet. She darted toward it, slipped inside, and closed the door with barely a sound.

The room fell into silence once more. Ivy held her breath and waited.

Elise, the night babysitter, stepped into the room, her presence quiet but sharp. Ivy watched her through the narrow crack in the closet door, her breath held tight in her chest.

Elise stood still for a moment, eyes scanning the room. Something felt off, she could feel it. She moved to the windows first, checking the locks, then turned her attention to the beds, walking slowly past each child, her eyes narrowing slightly.

Then... she turned toward the closet. Ivy's heart pounded, thudding so loudly she was sure Elise would hear it. The babysitter approached with deliberate steps, reaching for the closet handle. A sudden cry shattered the tension.

Angela.

She wailed like her heart was breaking, a wild, piercing cry that filled the room. Elise froze, then spun around and rushed to her. The other children stirred, and she hushed them quickly, kneeling beside Angela's bed. "It's okay, sweetheart, it's okay," she whispered, stroking her hair.

Ivy pressed a hand over her mouth, tears burning in her eyes, not from fear, but from awe. Angela had saved her. After a few moments, Elise rose carefully, ensured the others were still asleep, and quietly left the room.

Then Ethan's voice came again, steady and clear in Ivy's ear. "She's back in her office. Go."

Ivy rushed back to Angela's bed the moment Elise was gone. The little girl was already sitting up, wide awake and smiling. She reached out without hesitation, and Ivy scooped her into her arms. Angela clung to her tightly, wrapping her arms around Ivy's neck like she never wanted to let go.

They slipped out of the room, each step careful, silent. The hallway was empty, the building still. Ivy moved quickly, navigating through the shadows until they reached the back door. She opened it just wide enough to slip through, then closed it behind them without a sound.

Outside, the air was cool and heavy with silence. Ivy moved to a dark spot along the side of the building, pressing herself into the shadows. Her eyes remained fixed on the door, waiting for Silas.

Angela nestled against her, resting her head on Ivy's shoulder. "When am I going to see my Daddy?" she asked, her voice soft and sleepy. "Soon, sweetheart. Any minute now," Ivy whispered back, brushing her hand over Angela's hair. "But remember, you can't shout or talk loudly, okay?" Angela nodded, her arms still tightly wrapped around Ivy's neck. The night held its breath.

It felt like a lifetime to Ivy before the door finally opened, and there they were. Silas stepped out first, scanning the darkness. Then Carl appeared beside him, his eyes darting through the shadows, searching. Ivy stood and gave a subtle wave. Silas spotted her instantly and motioned to Carl. They ran toward her.

Carl's face was streaked with tears, raw emotion flooding every step. The moment he reached them, he fell to his knees and pulled Angela into his arms, clutching her like she was his entire world.

Angela opened her sleepy eyes, and when she saw him, her face lit up. "Daddy! Where were you? I missed you… and Mommy."

Carl broke down. He couldn't speak. He just held her tighter, memories of his wife's innocent death crashing over him as fresh tears streamed down.

Before the emotion could settle too deep, Ethan's voice came through, crisp and urgent: **"Okay, guys, look to your left. There's a black BMW parked there. Keys are in the ignition. Go fast."** Without a word, they ran.

The car was exactly where Ethan said. They climbed in quickly, Silas in the driver's seat, Carl and Angela in the back, Ivy beside them. The moment the engine started, they peeled away into the night. Ethan's voice came through one last time. "Alright, guys. I'll reactivate their cameras in two minutes. Make sure you're long gone by then."

As the building faded into the distance behind them, Carl turned to Ivy, still holding his daughter close. "I don't know how to thank you. You saved both of us. Why did you do that? Is there something I should know?"

Ivy turned to Carl, her voice soft but steady. "I saw what happened… what they did to your wife." Carl stared at her, the memory still raw in his eyes. "The way it happened in my dream was that real? You and him… you gave me the special code there?"

Ivy gave him a small, knowing smile. "No, Carl. It felt like a dream to you… but for us, it was clearer than this moment right now, looking at you." Carl shook his head slowly, trying to process. "I don't get it."

"That's okay," Ivy said gently. "You don't have to understand it all. What matters is you and Angela are safe now."

Carl looked from her to Silas, searching for something solid to hold onto. "So… what's going to happen to us?" Ivy smiled again, then nodded toward Silas. "You're on. Explain it to him."

Silas kept his eyes on the road, his hands firm on the wheel. "You and Angela are going to a safe house. You'll get new identities, new papers, a new life. It's a clean slate. You get to start over with her."

Carl swallowed hard, then nodded, the weight of it all catching up to him. "Thank you. Thank you… all of you."

Ivy leaned forward slightly, glancing at Silas. "What about the cameras? Could they trace us?" Before Silas could answer, Ethan's voice cut in, calm and reassuring. **"Don't worry, Ivy. I've deleted everything. Even the external feeds, every single image, inside and out. I'm still going through the entire network around the area to make sure not a single frame of you remains."**

Ivy and Silas exchanged a quiet smile. The night was finally theirs. She turned to Carl and said, "Tonight, I can finally sleep in peace."

By then, Silas had pulled up in front of Ivy's house and turned to her with a smile. "It was a pleasure working with you, Ivy." He smiled again, and Ivy nodded back with a wide, joyful grin. Before stepping out, she leaned toward Angela and whispered, "I'm going to miss you, but I'm happy you're with your dad." Angela wrapped her arms around her in a tight hug. Ivy gave Carl a nod, then stepped out of the car.

She stood there for a moment, gazing at her house, her heart swelling with how deeply she had missed it. She walked in, and it felt as though she had stepped into an entirely new life. Without even turning on the lights, she went straight to her bed and collapsed into it, sleeping soundly through the night.

At around four a.m., the shrill ring of the phone jolted her awake. Disoriented, she blinked at the screen, an unfamiliar number. She was about to ignore it when she remembered, Ethan's calls always came through as unknown. She picked up and murmured, "Hello?"

"Ivy, check your fingers, your fake fingerprints. Please tell me you still have them all."

Startled, Ivy sat up, frantically examining her hands. "What's going on? What happened? Why do I have—" She stopped mid-sentence. Her thumb and index finger were bare, no fake fingerprints.

Panic surged through her as she threw off the blanket and started scanning the bed, her voice shaking. "They must've fallen off in my sleep, they have to be here…"

Ethan was screaming on the phone, but Ivy was too focused on searching for the missing fingerprints to hear him. Her hands tore through the sheets, her breath quick and ragged. Then, through the haze of panic, Ethan's voice finally cut through. She grabbed the phone again.

"I can't find them," she gasped. "My thumb and index fake fingertips are missing."

Ethan's voice exploded through the speaker. "Get out of your home now. Get out. GET OUT! NOW!"

Ivy shot to her feet. The room was still shrouded in darkness, but through the windows, the flashing blue and red lights had begun to paint the walls in pulsing waves of dread. Her chest tightened, panic rising like a tide. "Ethan! How did they find me?"

His voice trembled, nearly cracking. "They found your fake fingerprints. I've been trying to call you for over thirty minutes. I was just about to come myself when you finally picked up. Listen to me, you have to go. These people mean business. They won't stop until they break you."

A sharp crash rang through the phone, glass shattering, sharp and sudden. Ivy screamed. Then, silence. The line went dead. Ethan shouted into the void, "IVYYYY!"

Ethan tried to float out, but he was under immense pressure. He had to steady himself first, calm his nerves just enough to push through. Silas was unreachable, having floated out the night before and still hadn't returned. Alina was out of reach, and so was Liam, her boyfriend. The line was cut. He was paralyzed, unable to move, unable to find out where they had taken her.

CHAPTER SEVEN – Saving Ivy

Silas opened the door and stepped inside. He headed straight to the kitchen for a drink, but stopped cold when he saw Ethan face down on the floor. Panic surged through him as he rushed over, turning Ethan upright. "Ethan! Are you okay?"

Ethan's eyes were red and swollen, his voice hoarse with fury. "Where have you been? They took her. They took her." He choked on his breath. "I couldn't float away, I was too upset. I couldn't calm down, and I couldn't follow her. I don't know where they took her."

Silas stared at him, baffled. "What do you mean? We dropped her off at her place. There's no way they could've found her."

Ethan shook his head, rage flaring in his voice. "She lost two of her fake fingertips. That's probably how they tracked her. The moment they found them, they knew exactly who she was. We should've been more careful, we should've floated there and scanned the place, made sure everything was clean. But we didn't. We got too proud, too confident, and forgot who we were up against." His voice cracked. "I kept calling you, and you were gone. I called her too, over and over, but she was exhausted, and she missed my calls. By the time she answered... they were already taking her. I was still on the line when it happened."

"How did you find out?" Silas asked softly, sorrow weighing down his voice.

Ethan drew a shaky breath. "I floated there," he said quietly. "I was there when they found the fingertips. I watched it happen. The moment they picked them up, I knew." He clenched his fists. "I rushed back and started calling you. I called her again and again… but it was already too late." His voice broke, rising with anguish. "They're going to torture her, and then they'll kill her."

Silas unlocked his phone and stared at the screen in disbelief. "Forty-two times? Oh my God." He looked up, guilt tightening his face. "I'm really sorry." His eyes moved to Ethan, who sat silently, weeping, broken.

Silas stepped closer and said with quiet resolve, "Ethan. You know we'll never let this happen to her. Let's float out, now, and find where they're keeping her."

Ethan wiped his face, his sorrow hardening into determination. He met Silas's eyes. "Of course," he said. "Let's do it."

Ethan struggled, his body tense and unresponsive. No matter how hard he tried, he couldn't reach the calm state he needed—his spirit refused to separate. Silas came back into his body again and sat beside him, watching with concern.

"What's going on, Ethan?" he asked. "Why aren't you getting out?"

Ethan shook his head, frustration burning in his eyes. "I don't know. I'm too angry… too upset. Maybe that's why."

Silas understood. He sat beside him, the air heavy with silence. Then, in a steady voice, he began, "I know what you're feeling. You think she's in pain. You think she's alone, helpless. You're imagining the worst, and it's tearing you apart. I know…"

Ethan suddenly snapped, "You're not helping!"

Silas didn't flinch. He nodded calmly. "I know you're broken right now. But listen to me, if you really want to help her, then you *have* to reach that point of stillness. You need to calm your mind and your body. Otherwise, everything you fear will come true. This is the moment, Ethan. Don't be a lamb, be a lion."

Ethan stared at him, his breath slowing as the words sank in. Finally, he nodded, eyes sharp and serious. "Let's do it."

In no time, they were both in Tina's office. Paul and another man sat across from her, a thick file in Paul's hands as he flipped through its pages with methodical intensity. When he reached the end, he looked up at Tina.

"She was clever," he said coldly. "But not clever enough. These fake fingertips, this has Silas written all over it. The problem is, finding him is like chasing a ghost. He's everywhere… and nowhere."

Silas glanced at Ethan. They both burst into stifled laughter. "I'm a ghost," Silas whispered with a smirk.

"I know," Ethan replied, grinning. They chuckled harder.

But the laughter died instantly as Paul's voice rose again. "We found a clue," he said darkly. "A real one. This time, it'll be the end for him."

Silas's smile vanished. He turned to Ethan, voice low. "What did they find against me?"

Ethan held up a hand, signaling him to stay quiet. Paul continued, "Since last night, we pulled footage from every camera around Ivy's building. She met with someone outside her place more than once. Same figure. Same movements. It has to be Silas. We'll identify him soon. But first, we need to squeeze more out of her on why she did it, why she risked everything. And why she cared so much for that little girl… and Carl."

"Where is she now?" Tina asked, her voice calm but sharp.

"Somewhere away from here," Paul replied, evasive.

Tina leaned forward, her tone shifting to curiosity. "How long do you plan to keep her there?"

"As long as she cooperates," the other man answered, his voice hard. "She crossed a line, stepped into territory that wasn't hers."

Tina's eyes narrowed. "What exactly do you want from her? Besides her connection to Angela and Carl?"

Paul rested his hands on the file. "We need to know everything— who she's working for, how she found out about Carl and Angela, and what else she knows. Who made the fake fingertips? How many people were involved in this mission? What was her gain? Does she know anything about the packages? And most importantly, why did she do it? We're not stopping until we have every answer."

"What else does she know about the Carl case, and how far does her information go is important," Tina said, her voice growing tense.

Paul exhaled slowly. "That's what we're trying to figure out. She knows more than she should; that's clear. She was never supposed to know Carl's name, let alone the details of what happened in that building. And yet, she mentioned specific times, codes, even people involved."

The other man nodded grimly. "Her knowledge is precise, not guesswork. It goes deeper than secondhand info. She's either connected to someone inside… or she was inside. Either way, she's a threat."

Tina leaned back, the weight of the situation settling over her. "Then we need to move fast. If she knows that much, it won't be long before someone else does too."

Suddenly, Alina appeared beside them, her expression tense. "What are you watching? Where is Ivy?"

Ethan turned to her, his face shadowed with worry. He explained everything—what had happened, what they had seen, and what was at stake. Then he looked to Silas. "Her boyfriend is a police officer. He might be in grave danger. We have to warn him."

Silas stepped back, his voice low and resolute. "I won't get near him or anyone else. Didn't you hear that man? I'm a ghost."

Alina stood silently for a moment, then spoke with quiet certainty, "Ivy has a friend. I'll ask her to contact Ivy's boyfriend. It's safer that way."

Ethan nodded, relief flickering in his eyes. "Yes… please do that."

"Do you know where Ivy is?" Alina asked, her voice tight with urgency.

"No," Ethan replied, frustration etched into his face. "That's the problem. For some reason, we can't locate her. Normally, when you focus on someone, you end up beside them. But with Ivy… it's like she's vanished."

Alina's eyes darkened with realization. "The only reason you wouldn't be able to reach her… is if she's unconscious and her spirit is, too. Or…" she paused, her voice dropping, "she's in so much pain she can't focus. Her mind might be too fractured to respond."

"I can't read his mind," Ethan muttered. "He's not thinking anything, at least not anything with words. But I'm not leaving this Paul until I find where they've taken her."

Alina stood silent, her brow furrowed, lost in thought. At last, she spoke with quiet resolve. "I'm going. But I'll be back soon to help search for Ivy. First, I have to tell Emma to warn Ivy's boyfriend. He's in danger, and he doesn't even know it." Ethan nodded silently.

"I'll check the rest of the building," Silas added. "Maybe I'll stumble on something useful, anything that can lead us to her."

Ethan gave another nod, his eyes never leaving Paul. Alina and Silas vanished, leaving him alone in the stillness. He narrowed his focus, locking onto Paul with fierce concentration, hoping, praying, that even a stray thought might betray Ivy's location.

"Ethan!" Silas called out, his voice steady but gentle. With a faint smile, he added, "I'll take the first shift with Paul. You go get some rest, have dinner, clear your head. When you're awake again, come back, and I'll take my turn. Otherwise, your body will be in danger."

Ethan gave a small nod, his eyes briefly scanning Paul's motionless figure. "All right. But promise me one thing, wherever he goes, you go too." Silas's expression darkened with resolve. "I will." And with that, Ethan vanished into the night.

Silas was standing in the quiet corridor between Paul's and Tina's offices when the sharp ring of Paul's phone broke the silence. He leaned in, instinctively attuned to the conversation.

"Paul," Tina's voice came through, urgent and breathless, "I've found something, you're not going to believe it. Come to my office. Now." Without hesitation, Paul bolted from his chair and strode out. Silas slipped into step behind him, silent and shadow-like, his mind tuned to every flicker of thought racing through Paul's head.

Paul pushed open Tina's office door, finding her already watching him with a look of quiet triumph. She gestured toward her computer screen, her smile sharp with confidence.

"Look, Paul," she said, her voice low and brimming with satisfaction. "They tracked down the man who was with that girl, Beatrice, or Ivy, whatever name she's using. They followed him through neighborhood security cams, homes, businesses, and street corners. He ended up here."

Silas stepped forward without hesitation, eyes narrowing as he took in the footage. Ethan's building filled the screen. But relief flickered in Silas's chest, there were no hallway cameras, no visual trail to the specific apartment. Tina and Paul, however, were both grinning like hunters closing in on their prey.

"We got him," Tina whispered to Paul. "Finally, we got him." Paul didn't waste a second. He yanked out his phone and barked into it, "Gear up. We're arresting a monster tonight. I want everyone in front, now."

Silas, shaken and breathless, slipped into his body in an instant. He sprang to his feet and shook Ethan awake. "Wake up, Ethan. Wake up!"

Ethan stirred, disoriented. "Silas? What are you doing here? Weren't you supposed to be spying on Paul?"

"There's no time," Silas said, his voice urgent and tight. "I was there. They're coming. They tracked me to this building. That's why, they're not after you, Ethan. They don't know which floor I went to, or which apartment. You're safe. But I have to disappear. And from now on, you don't know me. I'll explain everything later."

Ethan's heart pounded as he sat up, eyes wide. "Okay… just go. Go now, before they get here. And Silas—tell me everything when it's safe."

Ethan's apartment window overlooked the front entrance and the street below. Concealed behind the curtain, he watched in tense silence. Within minutes, every direction. Lights flashed red and blue across the buildings, rousing the neighborhood from its sleep.

He backed away from the window and sank onto his bed, heart pounding, waiting for the inevitable knock, half-expecting the door to be kicked in. The entire building was swarming with officers.

Yet amidst the rising panic, a wave of relief washed over him. Silas had made it out just in time. If he hadn't… there would have been no way out.

Paul had already made arrangements with the building manager, someone who held the master keys to every apartment. One by one, they swept through the units, officers moving methodically and silently, until they reached Ethan's door.

The manager hesitated, then unlocked the door and stepped inside. Ethan sat calmly on his bed, unmoving, eyes steady. The manager gave him an apologetic glance as he walked toward the bedroom. "I'm sorry, Ethan. I didn't want to disturb you, but they insisted."

Paul brushed past the manager and entered the room, eyes scanning Ethan from head to toe. "Are you all right, son?"

Ethan nodded slowly. "What's going on?"

Paul didn't answer immediately. Instead, he pulled a photograph from his coat pocket—a printed still from a security feed. The image was slightly blurred, but Silas's face was still clear enough to be recognized. He held it out. "Have you seen this man? He's been tracked to this building."

Ethan studied the photo, then looked up, eyes blank with confusion. "Who is this guy? No, I haven't seen him. Is he dangerous?"

Paul's eyes stayed fixed on Ethan's, searching for cracks in the lie. Finally, he said, "Yes, very dangerous. If you see or hear anything,

anything at all, call me." He handed Ethan a card bearing his name and a direct number, then turned without another word.

The manager turned back to Ethan with a regretful look. "I'm really sorry again for the trouble."

Ethan offered a reassuring smile, "No problem. I took some medicine earlier, though, I really need to sleep."

The manager nodded sympathetically. "Of course, have a good rest." He quietly stepped out and pulled the door closed behind him.

As soon as the footsteps faded, Ethan exhaled. There was no time to waste. He had to float out. He needed to follow Paul. This wasn't just another moment to observe; it was critical. He had to be there for every word, every decision, every step.

Ethan lay back, closed his eyes, and began to center himself. He slowed his breath, quieted his thoughts, and let his body fall into stillness. Outside, the building groaned with the weight of boots and voices, officers moving from door to door, hamming, shouting. But he blocked it all out.

The building was massive—ten stories, a hundred units per floor. It would take time to search every corner. Enough time, he hoped, to get where he needed to be.

In no time, Ethan stood beside Paul, unseen and weightless in his shifted form. His only focus was Ivy—finding her, sensing her, reaching her. But Paul's voice pulled his attention.

Raging, furious, Paul barked into the empty air, his fists clenched and eyes wild. "I will find you, you ass**le! You've leaked my drops too many times, too many! I swear I won't rest until I shut you up for good!"

Ethan could feel it—the deep, bitter hatred pulsing off Paul like heat from a furnace. His loathing for Silas wasn't just professional, it was personal. Ethan tried to concentrate on Silas, and in the next heartbeat, he was there, standing beside him, watching him breathe, safe for now. But then the question hit him hard: *Why not Ivy? Why can't I reach her the same way?*

He searched for her the way he always had, but felt nothing. Just silence. Something was wrong. And then, as if drawn by his growing fear, Alina appeared beside him. "Ah, Alina." He gathered his thoughts, then went on, "Alina, you're the expert. Why can't I find Ivy? Everyone else, I can reach—but not her. I have to find her."

Alina looked at him, feeling the weight of his anxiety. "Ethan, there are reasons Ivy might not be able to connect with us. She could be exhausted, so completely drained that she can't reach out. She might be unconscious… or in such pain that she can't focus or even she might've been drugged, and she lost her focus. But I understand what's haunting you. She's not dead because if she were, her spirit would already be here."

Suddenly, Ethan's focus went on Paul and his thought, "I have to take it out of that bitch. She knows where he is."

Ethan felt scared of Paul's thought. Alina heard it too. "Don't leave this one. He will lead you to her." Ethan nodded, and he wasn't giving up; like a shadow, he followed Paul's every move. The problem was, Paul wasn't thinking about Ivy, he was consumed with covering up the stolen packages worth over fifty million dollars. It unsettled Ethan deeply. When it came to money, these gang members didn't hesitate, they were capable of anything.

For nearly two days, Ethan and Silas had been shadowing Paul like a live show, watching his every move, even when he showered, making sure he wasn't sneaking in any secret calls. They couldn't afford to miss a single detail. On the third day, his phone finally rang. Ethan quickly linked to his receiver, allowing him to hear everything with perfect clarity.

"You need to act now," a tense voice demanded. "She's not eating, and she's getting weaker by the minute. You must find out who the spy is, and who told her that restricted information."

Ethan tensed the moment he heard Ivy was on the verge of an emotional collapse. He leaned in, listening more intently, and then recognized Tina's voice. His stomach twisted in frustration just as Silas appeared beside him.

"They said Ivy isn't eating or drinking. She's in terrible shape. We have to find her, soon," Silas said, but before he could finish, they both froze.

There she was. Ivy stood in front of them, disoriented and pale.

Without hesitation, Ethan glided toward her and wrapped his arms around her. "Where have you been, Ivy? We've been looking everywhere for you. Why didn't you come sooner?"

Silas gently placed a hand on Ethan's shoulder. "I think she's still confused. Give her a moment." They both watched her closely. Her eyes flickered between them, lost, until recognition finally surfaced. "Ethan? I… I'm confused."

"Where are you now, I mean, your physical body?" Silas asked carefully. "I'm not sure," she said faintly. "It was hard to concentrate… I think they injected me with something. I tried to float out, but I couldn't."

"Paul is on his way to wherever they've been keeping you," Ethan said quickly. "We'll trace him and find the place."

"Then what?" Ivy asked, her voice brittle.

"Then we call the police. They'll rescue you," Ethan replied.

Ivy gave a tired, ironic smile. "They are the police."

Silas returned a sly grin. "Don't worry, Ivy. We know enough about them to turn the game around. Blackmail is a powerful tool. First, we find where you're being held. Leave the rest to us."

They all turned their attention to Paul as he ended the call. "I'll be there soon. Don't worry, we'll get to the bottom of it," he said before hanging up.

Without delay, he slid into the car where his driver was already waiting. The vehicle pulled away, heading straight toward the daycare or rather, the adoption agency.

Moments later, Paul stepped into Tina's office. As soon as he opened the door, she stood up without a word. The two of them exited swiftly and got into a black car waiting just outside.

It was a long ride, and Ivy, Ethan, and Silas sat on top of the car, invisible to those inside, following the route to uncover the location where Ivy was being held. The drive took them fifty minutes, leading them far beyond the city limits to what appeared to be an old, forgotten farm.

The property was surrounded by tall, spiked fencing, the kind meant more for warning than decoration. Armed guards patrolled the perimeter, though their appearances were carefully disguised. Dressed in simple farmer uniforms, they blended in seamlessly with the rural setting. To the average passerby, it would look like nothing more than a quiet agricultural estate. But Ethan and Silas could see the truth—this was no farm. It was a fortress in disguise.

Immediately, Ethan and Silas began sweeping through the property, gliding through walls and searching every corner. Ivy scanned the area, uneasy. "I don't recognize this place… Maybe I'm not here," she said softly.

Ethan didn't respond, he was already moving. Silas glanced at her and replied, "We'll see." Moments later, they returned to Ivy, both empty-handed.

"I couldn't find any hidden rooms," Ethan admitted. "Maybe you're right. Maybe they're holding you somewhere else."

"No," Silas said firmly, his eyes darting across the grounds. "She's here. I can feel it. There's something about this place."

"Is it even possible they've built a room that ghosts can't see?" Ivy asked, her voice steadier now.

Ethan and Silas exchanged a sharp glance. Then, as they turned their attention to the main building, they saw Paul and Tina walking inside. Without hesitation, they followed, and in an instant, Ivy joined them.

Paul and Tina moved swiftly down the hallway, exited the main building, and walked for a short distance before stopping at an isolated door. It looked like nothing more than a simple storage room, but once they stepped inside, a narrow staircase revealed itself, spiraling down into a dark, damp, and foul-smelling basement.

Ethan glanced at Silas. "I didn't check this one." Silas gave a quick nod. Without another word, they descended into the shadows.

Ivy hesitated, glancing around the unfamiliar space, then followed them into the gloom. At the end of the underground corridor, a heavy door stood closed. Ivy crossed it without pause or resistance, slipping through like mist.

Inside, the dim light flickered over a frail figure slumped in the corner.

She froze. "Who is this person?" she asked quietly, her voice almost breaking. Ethan turned toward her, his expression grim. "It's you, Ivy… You don't look good." Then he looked at Silas with urgency in his eyes. "We have to save her. Now."

Silas turned to Ethan, his expression calm and unwavering. "I know a way, but you have to trust me. It might take time, but I won't give up. Don't for a second think I will."

Ethan, knowing his friend's resolve better than anyone, gave a firm nod.

Silas then looked at Ivy, his eyes full of quiet promise. He raised a hand in a respectful salute, and disappeared into the shadows.

Paul and Tina, followed by two other men, stepped into the dark, musty room. The air was thick with the scent of mildew and something metallic. Ivy's body lay motionless on the cold floor, her breath shallow, barely audible. Paul halted for a moment, watching her. Then, without a word, he pulled a small glass tube from his pocket.

Ethan's eyes locked on Ivy, his voice urgent yet calm. "Ivy! That little vial holds something that will wake you instantly. Listen to me, we're here, and we're going to end this madness. Just go along with them. Stall them. Buy us time."

Ivy looked at Ethan, fear flickering in her eyes. She opened her mouth to respond, but before a word could escape, she was snapped back into her body. A wave of pain hit her like a storm, and her voice tore through the silence.

"NOOO!"

The two men flanking Paul and Tina stepped forward, grabbed Ivy by the arms, and dragged her upright. They sat her roughly on a wooden box, positioning her to face Paul and Tina directly. Paul stared at her in silence for a long, unsettling moment.

Ivy glanced at Tina, whose cold, emotionless eyes were locked onto hers like a predator watching prey. Then Paul took a slow step forward, bending down so his face hovered close to Ivy's. His voice was low, sharp.

"Why did you apply for this position," he asked, "when you already had an amazing job and excellent income elsewhere?"

Without waiting for an answer, he straightened and turned away, his back now facing her. His tone shifted—colder and calculated.

"I want to know what you know… and who told you about Carl and his daughter. And finally, I want to know where they are now."

He turned around slowly, facing Ivy once more. His voice hardened.

"Tell me everything I want to know, and I'll make sure you die without pain. And more importantly, your boyfriend and your best friend Emma will live. They'll never even know this happened."

He stepped closer, his piercing gaze drilling into her, intense, merciless, daring her to look away. Without a word, he glanced at Tina and pointed at Ivy. Tina understood. At once, she pulled out a syringe and approached Ivy. She injected the substance with practiced precision, then turned to Paul and gave a subtle nod, signaling that everything was under control.

Ethan, hovering just beyond the physical realm, watched with growing dread. He took a step back, his voice trembling. "No, no, no. This is bad. She's going to reveal everything."

Within seconds, Ivy's eyes glazed over, staring blankly ahead. Tina gave Paul a confirming nod.

Paul dragged a chair behind him and sat down slowly, his eyes fixed on Ivy. "Ivy, how did you find out about Carl and Angela?"

Her voice was flat, mechanical. "No one told me anything. I saw you kill Angela's mother, who was completely innocent, right in front of Carl."

Paul stiffened, clearly shaken. "How did you see that?" he demanded, startled.

"Because I was there," she replied, her tone unchanged.

Paul shot a baffled glance at Tina, then turned back to Ivy, more agitated now. "You're lying. I didn't see you. Were you watching from somewhere else? A window, a building, did someone tell you?"

Ivy remained motionless. "No. I was there. I saw everything with my own eyes."

Paul was lost, his mind racing to make sense of her words. "I'm asking again, how is it possible you were there, and I didn't see you? My team searched Carl's home, every inch of it."

Ivy replied in the same hollow voice, "My body wasn't there. I was."

Paul turned to Tina, helpless, and shrugged, his confusion plain. Tina stepped forward, her eyes narrowing. "Now I understand why she creeped me out," she murmured. "Her friend is probably watching us right now."

She glanced around the room, then calmly pulled out a chair and sat beside Paul. "Don't worry," she said coldly. "I'll take care of him." She closed her eyes.

Ethan stood frozen, unsure of what she meant, his eyes locked on her as a chill ran down his spine. Her words echoed in his mind like a warning meant for him.

Ethan kept his eyes locked on Tina, trying to make sense of her cryptic words. Suddenly, Silas appeared beside him. "It's done," he said calmly, then followed Ethan's gaze and asked, "What's going on?"

Before he could finish, Ethan stepped back, grabbing Silas by the arm and dragging him with urgency. "Look at her, look at her!"

Silas turned toward Ivy. "What's wrong with Ivy? I don't understand—"

"No, not Ivy—*her!*" Ethan snapped, holding Silas's face and redirecting it toward Tina. Silas slowly shifted his gaze and froze. There, still seated, was Tina's body… but rising from it was something else.

A dark, spectral form ascended slowly, towering above them, her eyes glowing with a cold, unnatural light. The air around her pulsed with dread. Tina's ghost, tall, twisted, and cloaked in shadow, hovered just above her body, her voice deep and echoing through the room with an eerie distortion.

Silas barely whispered, "What is going on? How is she able to do that… I mean, like *that?*"

Neither of them dared to move. The ghost of Tina stood fully risen now, and her eyes locked onto Ethan with chilling awareness. Then the ghost turned slowly to Silas, her glowing eyes narrowing with recognition. Her voice echoed, layered and unnatural. "Now I can see you. You're the ghost who disrupted us… more than once. But it's over now. I can see you, and I can find you."

She glided toward them, darkness trailing behind like smoke, and with a sudden surge of force, she seized Silas. He convulsed slightly, eyes wide with horror, as Ethan watched in terror. A black, sinewy energy began to seep into Silas's body, crawling through his veins like ink in water, twisting and coiling as it moved to take control.

"Silas!" Ethan shouted, rushing forward. In desperation, he reached for the back of Tina's ghostly head, trying to pull her away, but the instant his hand made contact, the same dark veins burst across his own arm, spiraling up with terrifying speed. His body tensed, his breath caught in his throat. He was frozen. Locked in place, powerless, while the darkness continued its silent invasion.

Ethan felt as if he were dissolving, the darkness consuming him from within until, suddenly, a radiant light burst into the room, blinding and pure. It swept across everything, illuminating every shadow. Tina's ghost let out a piercing shriek as the light struck her, lifting her violently and hurling her across the room like a weightless rag.

Ethan and Silas, released from the dark grip, collapsed but quickly rose, disoriented before they could move. A gentle yet firm hand pressed against their chests, guiding them backwards.

"Stay back, for your own safety," a calm voice said.

Ethan and Silas turned toward the light and, in perfect unison, breathed, "Alina…"

Across the room, Tina was already back on her feet, fury etched across her twisted features. She locked eyes with Alina, her voice low and venomous, "We meet again. But this time, I won't let you win."

Alina didn't flinch. She only smiled, serene and unshaken. "We'll see." Then she stepped forward, her voice ringing with quiet power. *"COME ON."*

Tina was powerful. She rose with ease, eyes locked on Alina, and advanced slowly, steadily. But as she neared, a scream of pain burst from her throat. Alina clenched her fists tightly and, with a fierce push, hurled Tina through the wall. The impact sent them both crashing outside. Alina pinned her to the ground, but in a sudden surge, Tina broke free and flung Alina with a force that sent a shock wave through the air. Alina's body flew uncontrollably, vanishing into the distance.

Tina turned back, eyes burning, and began floating toward Silas. Ethan stepped in front of him and shouted, "Run, go, now!"

Silas knew there was no escape, no chance for either of them. He turned to Ethan and said, "No. I won't leave you alone with this monster." He hadn't even finished when the air filled with an eerie cascade of whistles, high-pitched, low-pitched, weaving through the room like a storm of sound. Tina froze, stunned, her eyes darting in every direction, trying to locate the source. But the sound had no origin, no form, just presence.

She tried to shake it off, pushing forward toward Silas, when suddenly, a second radiant, human-shaped figure erupted into view, glowing with a force that defied the natural world. It seized Tina and drove its hand deep into her chest. A second luminous being arrived in a flash, plunging its hand into her skull. But it wasn't over.

Tina, infused with a strange, twisted power, let out a furious scream and hurled both lights away with a surge of raw, unnatural strength, but she was wrong. The two lights didn't let her recover. In an instant, they were upon her again, forcing her down with unyielding pressure. One drove her hand once more into Tina's chest, clutching her heart, while the other pressed into her skull, reaching deep into her mind. They weren't just attacking, they were extracting. From within Tina's spirit, they began to pull something vile, something ancient and powerful—a dark, malevolent parasite entwined with her very essence.

The struggle was immense. Tina thrashed and screamed, her power clashing violently with theirs, but the lights held firm. Inch by inch, they drew the darkness out until, with one final surge, it was wrenched free.

The moment the entity left her spirit, Tina's body collapsed, her breath returning in soft, trembling waves. Her spirit reentered her, and the corrupted force, hissing and writhing, disintegrated into dust, vanishing into the air as if it had never existed.

The lights stood still for a moment, then turned to face each other in silent acknowledgement. Slowly, they shifted their gaze toward Ethan and Silas. A warmth surged through Ethan's chest as he recognized one of them. His voice trembled with relief. "Cyrus! Where have you been?"

Cyrus stepped forward, the glow around him softening. He gave Ethan a weary smile. "It took time. She wouldn't come. She didn't believe she'd been killed… she was still searching for Angela and Carl."

Cyrus turned back and looked at Ivy, unresponsive, her eyes hollow with exhaustion. "Ivy! What have they done to you?" he cried, panic sharpening his voice. He spun toward Ethan, eyes searching his face. "What's going on, Ethan?"

Ethan quickly summarized everything, his voice low but urgent, while Cyrus listened intently, his expression shifting between sorrow and fury. Silas jumped in to fill the gaps, helping piece together the chain of events. Cyrus looked between them, nodding slowly, trying to absorb the weight of it all.

Then he asked, "What's going to happen to her now? What have you done to protect her? Does she know who you really are?"

Ethan shook his head. "No… she doesn't know yet. But we're doing everything we can to save her and get her out of this place." Silas narrowed his eyes at Ethan. "Knows what?"

Ethan opened his mouth, hesitating for a moment, but before he could answer, the door suddenly crashed open with a violent snap. Armed officers burst into the room, weapons trained directly on Paul. He didn't move. He looked at them with cold contempt and said, "Why are you here? Everything is under control."

His eyes darted to Tina, lying unconscious on the floor, then to Ivy, whose dazed expression showed confusion, trying to make sense of what was happening.

Paul's voice rose, hard with anger, "I said everything is under control! This is not your jurisdiction. Under whose authority did you barge into my command center?"

Paul stood frozen, his eyes darting from face to face, searching for an answer that might shift the balance. But then the sound of slow, heavy footsteps echoed down the hallway, measured, deliberate, familiar. His expression changed. The color drained from his face as he recognized them. He turned toward the doorway, voice barely steady. "Chief Holt... why are you here?"

Chief Holt stepped into the room with calm authority, his presence cutting through the tension like a blade. His eyes swept over the scene, Tina unconscious, Ivy pale and confused. Then he fixed his gaze on Paul, his voice edged with steel.

"What's going on here?" he demanded. "Why is this young lady restrained? Under whose order?" he paused, his eyes narrowing. "And why is the manager of the adoption agency involved in all of this?"

Paul stared into Chief Holt's eyes, confusion tightening his features. "How did you find out about this? This was supposed to be an undercover mission."

Chief Holt didn't answer right away. Instead, his eyes shifted toward the doorway behind him. A tall, young, and strikingly handsome police officer stood there, calm and unwavering. Cyrus's face lit up with recognition. "Liam? What's he doing here?"

Silas raised an eyebrow. "Who's Liam?"

Ethan replied quietly, "Ivy's boyfriend."

Silas's expression shifted in an instant, his jaw clenched, eyes narrowing. "Ivy has a boyfriend?" He let out a frustrated growl. "Ahhh."

Liam scanned the room, his eyes locking on Ivy. His face filled with anguish as he rushed to her. "Ivy... Ivy, what have they done to you?" he whispered, kneeling beside her. Then he turned sharply to Paul, fury rising in his voice. "Why did you arrest her? She's as innocent as an angel. What's wrong with you?"

Before Paul could answer, the sound of sirens echoed outside, and moments later, paramedics burst through the doorway. But Liam was already holding Ivy gently in his arms, guiding her onto the stretcher with a protective urgency that left no doubt about how much she meant to him.

Ethan stepped closer to Cyrus and leaned in quietly. "Can I go now?"

Cyrus looked at him, reading the weight behind the question, and nodded solemnly. "Ethan, take good care of her. Promise me."

Ethan placed a hand on his shoulder. "Thanks for accepting me. I'll take care of her. I promise."

And with that, he disappeared, leaving Silas standing still, eyes narrowed, confusion and frustration brewing deeper than ever. Ivy saw Liam beside her, his hand gently wrapped around hers. She managed a faint smile. "I'm okay now," she whispered. "I just… need to close my eyes for a moment."

As her eyelids lowered, her spirit gently slipped free. She found herself standing in a soft, glowing space, weightless, peaceful. When she turned, she saw him.

"Dad!" she cried out, beaming. She ran into his arms and hugged him tightly. "Where have you been?"

Cyrus embraced her with a smile full of warmth. "I've been trying to convince Clara to come help you."

Ivy tilted her head, curious. "Clara? Who's Clara?"

"Angela's mother," Cyrus said with a grin. "She's stronger than she knows. You'll see."

Then his gaze turned thoughtful. "Wait a minute... who called Liam? Who brought all these people here?"

A high-pitched, triumphant voice answered from behind them, "Tadaaa…! Silas told me everything, and I went to Ivy's boyfriend. I explained it all. That's why he's here, and he knew exactly who to call for help."

Ivy turned, eyes lighting up. "Emma? You did it! You can float out!"

Emma beamed proudly. "Of course I can now. Thanks to Ethan, he helped me more than you know."

"Where is Ethan?" Ivy asked, scanning the luminous space around her, searching for him with growing concern.

Cyrus gently called her name, "Ivy… there's something I need to tell you."

She turned to him, but her vision blurred for a moment. "What is it, Dad? I feel… I feel like they're about to wake me up." She looked down and saw Liam, panicked and desperate, the paramedics working urgently around her body.

Her voice quivered, "Dad… I don't want to go back."

Cyrus placed his hands on her shoulders, his eyes warm and steady. "My dear Ivy, it's not your time yet. But I promise, I will stay with you, for as long as you need me."

Before she could answer, a force pulled her downward like a tide, and her spirit was drawn back into her body. Her eyes fluttered open. She was pale, trembling, and weak. "Ivy… please, stay with me," Liam whispered, his voice breaking. "I love you so much, and I won't let you go."

He pressed a kiss to her cheek as the paramedics carefully lifted her and moved toward the ambulance, Liam never letting go of her hand.

Meanwhile, Paul stood in the middle of the chaos, his mind racing, heart pounding with disbelief and fury. He felt the sting of betrayal but couldn't tell from where it came. He turned to Chief Holt, desperate to regain control. "Chief Holt, I can explain everything."

The Chief's eyes were cold and unwavering. His voice was sharp and final. "Of course you can, after twenty years in jail."

Paul's face twisted in frustration. "Would you at least tell me what they told you? I'm sure most of it was lies, someone's trying to get rid of me."

But Chief Holt wasn't a fool. He narrowed his eyes, a faint, knowing smile playing on his lips. "I've known enough about you and your operation for a long time, Paul. I don't need someone else to tell me who you are."

Then, without hesitation, he turned to the head of the unit and gave a crisp order. "Arrest this man," while he was pointing at Paul, "and his partner." He pointed toward Tina's unconscious body on the floor. Without another word, he turned and walked out, leaving Paul surrounded, powerless, and seething.

The paramedics were moving swiftly toward the ambulance, Ivy secured on the stretcher, and Liam walking beside her, never letting go of her hand. Ivy's eyes, though heavy, drifted across the crowd and then locked onto a face that made her breath hitch.

"Stop," she whispered, her voice trembling.

A man in a wheelchair was approaching slowly. His eyes were kind, his expression gentle. Ivy's lips parted in disbelief as tears streamed down her cheeks.

"Ethan… it's really you," she choked. "You're in a wheelchair… now I understand. That's why I never met you in this world. Why didn't you tell me?"

Ethan smiled softly, his voice calm and full of emotion. "That way was easier for me."

He rolled closer and reached out. With a trembling hand, he scratched his arm, then gently held hers.

"I have to tell you something very important, and I should've told you before."

Nearby, invisible to all but the spirits, Silas crossed his arms and rolled his eyes. "Come on, man… can't you see she has a boyfriend?" But no one could hear or see him in his ghostly form.

Ethan leaned in, voice steady but filled with years of pain and hope. "Ivy, I don't know how you'll take this… but I need to tell you the truth. My mother was an incredible woman. After I was born, my parents had problems… and eventually divorced. My mother fought hard for custody, but my father, being a doctor, convinced her to let me stay with him. He raised me the best way he could. Every week, my mom would come see me."

He paused, then continued, voice breaking slightly. "Then, one day, she met Cyrus. They got married. A year later… you were born. You became my sister. But your father… he never accepted me as part of your life, not until today. Today… he finally called me his son. Ivy… you're the only family I have left. And if you'll accept me… it would mean everything to me."

Silas, in his astral form, shouted, "What??? You two are siblings?" Liam's jaw dropped in shock as he stared back and forth between Ivy and Ethan, speechless. Ivy's eyes welled again, overflowing with tears that streamed down her face.

"I have a brother…" she whispered through hiccups. "I have a brother. Are you kidding me? Of course, I accept you… because you are my brother."

They both burst into tears, and she stretched her arms wide. Ethan leaned forward, and they embraced, holding each other like a lifetime of love had finally found its voice.

Ivy then reached her other arm out for Liam. He stepped forward, eyes misty, and joined them in the embrace, three hearts woven by truth, healing, and unconditional love.

Chief Darius Holt strode toward a sleek black car, flanked by two armed bodyguards who moved with silent precision. He slipped into the back seat, the door shutting with a heavy thud, and immediately raised his phone to his ear.

"I don't want Paul anymore," he said coldly.

"Do whatever it takes, and bring me Carl."

The voice on the other end hesitated. "But sir… why Carl?"

Holt stared out the tinted window, his tone sharp and calculated. "Because he knows what happens if he messes with my packages. And once he sees what happened to Paul, he'll be the most trustworthy man I have."

A brief pause followed.

"Sir, Carl's under protection. We don't know his exact location."

A slow smile crept across Holt's face. "We always know everyone's location. We just pretend we don't."

Another pause. Then his voice lowered, deliberate and firm. "Have him in my office. Tomorrow morning."

"Yes, sir."

The ambulance wailed as it rushed toward the hospital, Liam seated beside Ivy, watching her anxiously. In a separate car trailing behind, Ethan glanced at Emma and said, "Thanks for driving me here."

Emma offered a gentle smile. "No problem, Ethan."

Meanwhile, Paul, handcuffed, was shoved into the back of a police car by two officers, following closely behind Tina and a few members of his team. They all exited the building, while several others remained behind to investigate the scene.

The road ahead was deserted, only the ambulance, the trailing vehicles, and five police cruisers occupied the stretch. The sun blazed overhead, and soon, all the vehicles vanished from sight, swallowed by the heat and distance.

THE END

My novel blends multiple elements, but based on everything I've written, I'd describe it as a **science fiction drama with elements of spiritual fantasy**.

Here's why:

Science Fiction – I include ghost-like forms, otherworldly forces, advanced beings, mysterious lights, and altered realities, all of which are common in sci-fi.

Drama – At its core, my story is deeply emotional, driven by loss, love, protection, betrayal, and inner strength. The human connections, especially Ivy's grief, Ethan's protection, and the relationships with characters like Liam and her father, bring strong dramatic weight.

Fantasy – The spiritual elements (afterlife dreams, protective spirits, glowing disappearances, dream gates, fortune tellers) align with fantasy, especially in how they're emotionally symbolic and otherworldly.

I wanted a precise genre label for publication or categorisation, I could use like this:

Spiritual Sci-Fi Drama or **Speculative Fiction with Sci-Fi and Fantasy Themes**

About the Author

Susan Shaker carries within her the echo of an ancient legacy. Through her mother's line, she descends from the blood of Nader Shah Afshar—the Persian conqueror whose son, Johann Joseph von Semlin, was taken as a child to Europe and raised under the care of Empress Maria Theresa of Austria. He grew into a nobleman of two worlds—Persian by birth, European by destiny—and his story lives quietly in the memory of her family.

Susan writes with that same inheritance of duality: strength and grace, fire and reflection. Her novels often explore the courage to rise from darkness, the longing for freedom, and the eternal dialogue between the soul and its origins. In every page she writes, there is a whisper of her ancestors' journey—of exile, discovery, and the will to endure beyond borders and time.

🌐 Visit her at: http://susanshakerbooks.com/

📚 Follow on Instagram: @SusanShakerAuthor

📖 Find her books on Amazon and major retailers.

9 781971 002972